UNDERCURRENTS

Also by Marie Darrieussecq

Pig Tales
My Phantom Husband

UNDERCURRENTS

A NOVEL

MARIE DARRIEUSSECQ

Translated by Linda Coverdale

THE NEW PRESS

NEW YORK

Originally published in France as *Le Mal de mer*
by P.O.L. Paris, 1999
Published in the United States by The New Press, New York, 2001
Distributed by W. W. Norton & Company, Inc., New York

LIBRARY OF CONGRESS CATALOGING-IN-PUBLICATION DATA

Darrieussecq, Marie.
    [Mal de mer. English]
    Undercurrents : a novel / Marie Darrieussecq ; translated
by Linda Coverdale.
       p. cm.
    ISBN 1-56584-627-3 (hc.)
    I. Coverdale, Linda.   II. Title.

   PQ2664.A7214 M3513 2001
   834'.914—dc21   00–061275

The New Press was established in 1990 as a not-for-profit alternative to the large, commercial publishing houses currently dominating the book publishing industry. The New Press operates in the public interest rather than for private gain, and is committed to publishing, in innovative ways, works of educational, cultural, and community value that might be deemed insufficiently profitable.

The New Press
450 West 41st Street, 6th floor
New York, NY 10036
www.thenewpress.com

Printed in the United States of America

2   4   6   8   10   9   7   5   3   1

I live by the ocean
and during the night
I dive into it
down to the bottom
underneath all currents
and drop my anchor

this is where I'm staying
this is my home

Bjork Gudmundsdottir

UNDERCURRENTS

It's a mouth, half open, breathing, but the chin, nose, and eyes are no longer there. It's a mouth bigger than any mouth imaginable, rending space in two, expanding it, so that you must swivel your body in a semicircle to try seeing it all. The noise—the breathing—is tremendous, but most of all you don't expect it: you climb up the dune, you struggle to haul your feet up the slope, for a while you're concerned only with this suction beneath the sand, and in one swoop space explodes, you've looked up and the top of the dune has fallen deeply away, something like two colossal arms opening wide, but that's not exactly right—it's not welcoming, it's rather that you have no choice, the way you'd fall off a building or a monument without a parapet. It's hard to visualize the edge of this thing, hard to decide precisely where it is, how far away. Before, you were going up the dune, already hearing the noise but not feeling anything on your face yet, leaning toward the sand, in the cold dry smell of the sand, and then the noise spread out, as if overflowing even behind your head, a three-hundred-sixty-degree noise, whereas the sea is straight ahead, blowing in your face, patting away the sweatiness of the climb with a raspy breath, salty but not humid, dried by the still scorching breadth of the beach.

She goes over the climb in her thoughts, to recover that moment (even though the sea is there in front of her and fills her whole head), to relive that moment when space split asunder, sprang out to the sides, and liquefied into this black mass, thrusting back the edges of the sky and dissolving them, drinking them, breathing through millions of red slits opening and closing on the motionless black mass, through millions of little mouths on the enormous closed black mouth where a pale gleam lingers at the place where the sun waggled its tongue. To rediscover that moment when, all of a sudden, the dune became the sea, you would have to go back down, start all over, pretend to have forgotten and close your eyes, opening them again only at the top, absorbing the shock without flinching, forcing your body to stand there facing the void. But the sun has set, the sky overhead has turned black and is slowly descending, folding the sea over on itself, and that's it for the first time, now she has seen the sea.

Her face is as if washed with it, opened up, and her mother believes that—that you can tell from people's faces, especially children's, who has seen the sea and who has not: those who must have welcomed the sweep of the sea into their eyes (crashing all the way to the backs of their skulls, it empties them out, in a way), and those who were able only to dream it, from pictures or words, those who have tried, confusing the sea and infinity, to keep adding a little bit more to the image, telling themselves that even beyond, still farther, without end, the sea goes on . . . when it's not that at all, when compared to galaxies, the sea is minuscule. She passes her hand over the little girl's face, a round face, indistinct, made even less distinct by the impact of the sea: a broadening of the cheeks, the gaze; the fluttering of metamorphosis beneath the skin; a boundless childhood, distended, pelagic. They would have to stay there, right there in that moment, to let it last as long as that grandeur requires. She feels, rolling beneath her fingertips, the sand grains that microscopically graze the surface of this face, until the little girl shakes herself and blinks, perhaps to recover that first moment of the sea, or to get rid of the sand and doubtlessly, impatiently, the hand.

She leaves the child on top of the dune. She feels something like relief, a pause; the intuition that she can leave her there, busy with the sea, eyes straining from their sockets; in the pointlessness of fishing poles, sinkers, floats, and even buckets and shovels. She won't rush down to the beach straightaway, she won't run off to drown in the waves; unlike logs blazing in fireplaces or outdoor bonfires, the sea does not cozy up to us, it doesn't crackle within arm's reach: you look at it a long time before it dawns on you that you can touch it. She opens the car trunk. The tent is there, where they leave it between vacations; she takes the sweaters, the blanket, the Tupperware container of hardboiled eggs, the flashlight. She's much calmer than she was on the freeway. She has this feeling now of having thought of everything. The flashlight works, spotting heather at the foot of the trees, and craters of sand. The ten thousand francs are in her pocket; she must stop being afraid that they'll fall out, that the wind will snatch them away, that the child will play with them. The wad of bills is already a little thinner; she was given coins as change from the orange juice and the roll. Slowly, she retraces her steps; she has the eggs, the blanket, they're all set, that's what they're going to do: eat and sleep here. The little girl forms a slight bump on the crest of the dune, a hummock haloed in dark purple. Too recently raked by the sun for stars to be peeking through so soon, the sky behind her is tarry, unless that's the ocean; she has climbed high enough to see it, she has passed that point where the noise seems to issue no longer—muffled—from the dune, but from all of nocturnal space. She would like to show that to the child, and dreading a struggle, she wraps her in the blanket; she should see that, the way the horizon melts into the sea because eyes seared by the sunset can no longer tell sky from water, or because at the sun's zenith and at twilight there are, as is said of a tide on the turn, slack moments of light: one white and the other black, one diurnal, the other nocturnal, eroding by turns the heights or the horizon; so it is at that dim hour, when the day-laden sea swells and cracks, and when fingers swept through hair produce a humming and electric sound.

On one side she senses the presence of the trees, their black crowns; on the other, this emptiness, also black, but flat, immense, into which the body leans, held back at the neck by that scratchy blanket. Her mother holds her so close that her buttocks are lifted slightly off the sand. She's tired, and would like to go home and sleep. The red mouths have vanished. If she wriggled free, if she got up and ran, she would realize, but too late, that one side is missing: her leg would slip or be dislocated or shrink at one go, she would teeter on a stump, un-supported, toppled over by this missing ground or foot. The eggs form a dry paste on her tongue: the white—smooth—and the yolk—earthy—mix to-gether as they stick to the roof of her mouth; saliva isn't flowing quickly enough, it's as if egg, egg paste, is what her mouth is secreting now, a wax smeared over her gums and gullet. On the freeway, she swallowed the roll down with the orange juice, but it seems her mother didn't think to bring along any water. Asking her for some is a delicate proposition, assuming any sound could still percolate through the egg; she's easily upset, she might start shouting. The egg in the throat descends, distending the lining, requiring faster breathing and giving the impression it's going to get stuck there, where the neck joins the thorax, beneath that fold emphasized by the blanket as though she were nothing but a doll with a cloth body, a stitched bag that was going to swallow soon but inside which the puppeteer's hand, as everyone knows, moves to mimic living organs. Her mother shakes her and she is hollow once more, resonant, famished; as she was on the freeway before the roll, in the car that seemed (once the joy of sitting in front with the seat belt under her chin had worn off) so different, facing the windshield full of that straight, unfamiliar road, which did not lead back home. In the gleam of the flashlight, her mother going down the dune again is long and black like the pines, a pine with arms and legs, releasing pale beams of light fanning out into the underbrush.

She has forgotten the water; there isn't anything else in the trunk except the tent and the schoolbook bag. She could so easily have asked her mother for some water when she picked up the child, but with what excuse—a Thermos, a bottle, for a trip supposedly of three suburban streets, lasting five minutes? Farther on, she never thought to buy any, for from the very first kilometers of sunshine, a migraine—exhausting and familiar—had taken up all the space, leaving no room for other feelings. That's it, it has got her again: at the left temple, throbbing beneath the bone; a single point, fixed, small, a pellet you could simply tear out, but its transmitting range encompasses her isolated and ringing skull. As on the radar screen of a submarine, its beam sweeping over its target of torpedoes, the pain glows more fiercely with each heartbeat, her body reeling from the impact—her whole body and not simply her head: a staggering shock. She would have to leave herself completely behind, like a shed skin, since she generates, like people exposed to atomic radiation, an aura that is consuming her. She lowers the hood of the trunk gently; it's not enough, you have to slam it. She feels her energy drain away. Up there, on the dune, the child doesn't seem to be looking anywhere; all you can make out, against the nocturnal luster of the sea, is a hint of her profile, slightly inclined, a medallion of indifference (and yet the sea for the first time, the surprise of bringing her to the shore, a five-hour drive away . . .). Taking the tent, she moves forward, her head enormous around the tiny central point of the migraine, her body snapping in pain like a sheet on a clothesline; what is scouring her out like this, hurtling around freely inside her, certainly cannot be contained within her body but must surely—how to put it—be audible, visible, at least noticeable, giving off light, and she's being tracked at a distance, as if she were lugging a transmitter; moreover the tent, the blanket, and the book bag are booby-trapped. She hesitates, and her feet slip on the steep sand. But no one could have anticipated, imagined, forewarned; no one can follow them.

She's not entirely sure that it's the sea. She would have liked some advance notice, to prepare herself; it's a little like the day her mother took her to the movies for the first time, and she was frightened, even if she now enjoys reviewing in her head that moment when her mother parks in an unfamiliar spot, not very far from the house, but on a strange street, one that looks like the street the house is on but that opens, through a big door, onto a deep hole, with a flight of stairs, where a giant maw grooved with red arches gapes in turn, making her scream in terror from the audience; now, though, she'd like to start over again, now that she knows, slipping once again into the darkness and even into the belly of the whale, laughing at that dizziness and then clinging to the raft with Pinocchio. She thought today, as she has often hoped, that they were going to the movies, she really believed and hoped so since the streets weren't exactly those leading home, because they were leaving grandmother's not by following the canal but by turning left, toward the boulevard, the one they go down, usually, on market days. But the town got bigger. From the car windshield streamed new streets, at the end of which burst a sheaf of other streets, carving out other directions; the windshield is starred from all those streets that turn, split up, spread out, framed for a moment in the side and rearview mirrors and zigzagging with pedestrians, then gliding smoothly, walls washed, edges erased, streets that divide and reopen, constantly shifting the depth of space until they gather together in a gray trench, long and straight, fluted with slits and roughened with rhythmic white. She's not entirely sure that it's the sea—perhaps she slept a while before arriving on these dunes; she's missing a stage, something between the grandmother, the streets, the freeway and the roll, and then the sea. She sat down in the front seat, wondering about the movies, and what do you know, the proud streets were brought low, replaced by greens and yellows, leaning telephone poles, a flat, swiftly flowing landscape; then something soft oozes into the car, as though wafted in by the shimmering blacktop, or the heat; she sinks slowly into the seat as the foam rubber beneath the fabric gradually gives way, swallowing her from the rear, a deglutition, hesitant velvety lips that suck in, then half let go, following the cadence of the road. She opens the window all the way when her mother stops to fill the tank and the smell of gas seeps into her stomach. A little farther along is the shopping center, where her mother spends so much time buying her a snack. The parking lot is almost empty. The air between the cars is warped. She slides over on the seat, stretches her feet toward the pedals, tries turning the wheel. The mirages tremble. The store windows blow bubbles of sunlight. The shopping carts cut cubes from a kind of gray jelly that quivers between the metal bars, bounces off the asphalt. Forms slowly thicken, legs take shape where only gray ripples floated before, eyes and nostrils poke through in faces. Cars drive off. She wants so much to cry it's becoming unbearable. Her mother is huge all of a sudden, completely covering the windows. Then the windshield fills with white sky as crash barriers rush by, rising and falling. Her mother is practically lying across her lap, acrobatically closing the window, driving with one hand; her hair is loose and seems somehow naked, brushing against her, bleached in light streaks amid the darker mass. And now she's on this dune, her mouth plastered shut with egg. Shouldn't the sky be blue, the waves white, the horizon marine and sprinkled with sails? The sea, if it is the sea, appears to have poured down from the black sky, capsizing into a liquid night, the weighted base of a culbuto world that keeps the sky in balance. It laps gently; without that faint noise you wouldn't see it, you'd feel only that heaviness that won't let you pluck your feet from the sand and run; that low-lying mass, that tremendous condensation of shadow, beneath a sky hissing with the wind that separates them.

Occasionally, there where a breeze suggests a line perhaps a touch grayer, a fold smoothed out immediately, big glimmering bubbles seem to surface, showing you where the sky is, blue globes that are soon engulfed again, leaving briefly behind only a dull fluorescence, no doubt from jellyfish; perhaps, tomorrow, without going too close to the water's edge, she'll be able to point them out to the child; she thinks she remembers that in daylight, jellyfish—this kind, at least—look like bowler hats, as if men were strolling around beneath them. That's what she would need: to float about, let the waves wash through her; the migraine would melt, dissolving in the flood; her brain would become a bluish globule, empty, aqueous and soft, that would bear her body as though she were sleepwalking under the sea. In the meantime the tent must be set up; the stars have not come out, and it might rain.

She holds the tent pegs carefully, between her tightly closed hands. There are twelve of them: she hasn't lost a single one since last year. The tent is spread out on the sand for the moment, a big blue bag that flutters and takes unexpected shapes. The year before, when all three of them went to the mountains, she was already in charge of the pegs but the method seemed more reliable: her father inside with the tent poles, her mother outside with the cords, the two of them shouting, but when the tent finally went up, revealing this hollow inside, within cloth panels that had been so flat before, the night became inhabitable. She slept sandwiched by both of them, her head at their necks and her feet by their knees, wedged between two poles; by stretching out her toes she could make the entire tent shimmy. Dreaming sheep tinkled little bells. Through the blue folds, made even bluer by the darkness, you could make out the stars, bright halos in the woven cloth, revealing the woof and weft as if through a magnifying glass. Fabric, bells, a mountain stream, the night: things were close, and the tent formed the membrane, within and without, between her own skin and the world, just thick enough to contain, amid the smells of grass and mildew, the warmth of their breathing. The tent is heaving on the sand now, reminding her of a cat that was shut up in a bag and dropped from a balcony during a birthday party. The pegs won't hold well in the dune; her father used a hammer for the hard soil of the mountain. Something under the trees wails like a saw, with rufflements of wings. Then she sees the blue fabric above her head. Little bells still seem to be ringing in her ears, but the stars aren't shining through, as if the cloth were sheathed by a second roof, black and opaque, which must be envisioned (when it trembles, rent by the wind, in rapid stripes) as suspended from the shadow of the pines. The sand hums, from periodic impacts. She isn't touching anything, she isn't moving, the ground is level, but she keeps tipping. And now her feet stick out beyond the poles.

She has the ten thousand francs, in her pocket; she touches the roll of bills and the few coins. She didn't feel up to getting undressed, or to making the child do so, either. They haven't brushed their teeth; anyway, there isn't any water. After all, perhaps it will be cold tonight, and she'll be happy the child is sleeping in her clothes, as the blanket is thin. She could have bought a sleeping bag and some extra sweaters this afternoon, but didn't think of it. That's because of the migraine.

Next to the gas station she saw first that sign outside
the pharmacy, then the white smock, behind a counter.
It's a nuisance to get out the whole wad of money, it
looks strange, obviously. The Paracetamol, taken immediately, seems to absorb the most searing part of the
pain. She can still see the car clearly, and the child as
well: hands gripping the steering wheel, she's bound to
be imitating the engine noise with her mouth. After
buying the snack, she'll still have about 9,950 francs
left. It's a big supermarket, where the door opens and
closes with an electric eye; when she walks into its little
red gaze, gusts of cold air bathe her in an icy breath.
Leave the child, go out the other side, someone will
find her, obviously, and she—ten thousand francs, a
plane ticket. She walks through the red eye, wearing
just that light sundress; the little wheels squeak, the
entrance gate is there, hip high, two automatic doors
painted with white arrows; the cookie and soda shelves
are probably far away at the other end. Light falls
from overhead in the supermarket, a light that has
passed through windows, yellow and exhausted, with
blotches that must be leaves or insects made gigantic
by their shadows. People push past her; each time they
open, the arrows point to the invisible back of the
store, then re-close to indicate the tiny target at their
junction, a point one centimeter wide; she looks away
and finds herself facing the small shops. The Danish

pastries have a greasy sheen; she asks for a roll and an orange juice; against her belly she feels the burning hot roll and the chilled can, although she would have preferred a bottle for the child. Now night has fallen and is creaking everywhere. The roof of the tent sags: she managed to drive in the pegs but couldn't tighten the cords enough. She might have thought for a moment, one moment, about what they needed, even if it was only water. That limp blue material above her face, almost touching it—she could cry.

This morning in school no one was talking about vacation yet. The teacher had just handed out permission slips for the end-of-the-year trip, she wants both parents' signatures. She put the slip in her schoolbook bag, but now that she thinks about it—did they bring it along, from grandmother's? She stretches and wiggles her toes, discreetly, knees drawn up to her stomach; the ground is hard, compacted. If she moves, she feels sand grains slipping away beneath the plastic, out from under her, a silent fall, and then a lump, a ridge, some cement that solidifies and bruises. Her back is itching; insects, maybe, scrambling around, struggling beneath her weight, tunneling, scratching their carapaces on the sand grains. She'd have to go outside, very quietly, find the car keys, and rummage around for the book bag. A

tingling climbs her cheek; her muscles tighten like rubber bands. Her mother seems to be sleeping. Spiders,
coleoptera, stag beetles, and earwigs are everywhere;
the sand is so fluid you need only dig between two
roots, let the warm grains shower down on you, and
mingle your six or eight legs with the six or eight legs
of your nest mates, in order to doze off lazily, conscious only—sweetly, erratically—that all the wing
sheaths have begun to stir, without your knowing anymore whether it's you or one of your neighbors whirring like that, fast asleep.

The night is purple through the blue fabric, the
Moon must have risen; now only the branches—or
rather, the spliced crowns of the pines—weave black
cables around the tent, and something mauve hoots
along with the rasping of the crickets: an owl, a night-
bird; she turns her head slowly toward the child, whose
eyelids are squeezed shut, her small fists rubbing
against her cheeks. She appears to be asleep. She picks
up one of her wrists, so slender, and unfolds the fingers
with her own; the silly thing is still biting her nails. The
owl and the crickets have stopped screeching. She can't
manage to fall asleep; not that she was really counting
on sleeping, but she would have liked at least to take a
little breather from the migraine. Things are creeping
beneath the tent; inexplicably, they stop moving, buried in the ground, imperceptible at a dead set. The

wind slips through the trees, almost silently, skimming the dune, skimming the tent, as if the world were as sleek as pine needles. The mass of sand doesn't give beneath her back, pulls her down and holds her, limbs, chest, neck, head. The sound of the sea grows louder, filling in those holes in space where both birds and insects have gone quiet. Yet what she hears is like an exaggeration of the silence, a liquid, material silence, underlying the tick-tock of the blood in her skull and the irregular jolts of a branch swishing, bark peeling away, the crunch of a pile of pine needles; the ultra-soft whisper of the sand, perhaps, beneath the step of a prowler. She listens, and the silence grows even more vast, filling the tent brimful, throbbing at her eardrums. The steps draw closer and she holds her breath—it's a respiration that glides over the sand, in waves: she loses it if she listens for it (then the migraine pounds louder), and finds it again with the sea, the rustling, the sudden crescendos, so that sometimes, instead of this one distinct footfall, it seems that the dune and the forest are on the move. She opens the zipper; the night pours in, enormous and violet, streaked by the pines. The air is cool, the sand grows cold beneath her feet. No one can find them.

She called her several times, mom-my: she watches her move along the top of the dune, the black shape of the dress opening and closing on the sandy slope; she's going to go down the other side. The tent opening is flapping, scraping the zipper against a pole; the fabric slithers, puffs up, collapses. The pines stand still, on the alert. Somebody's going to come, with a knife, big boots that will make deep puddles of blood, and all anyone will find will be thick black crusts; there, over by the bristling underbrush, something is moving that is neither holly nor heather: a spine, fur, eyes, a quadruple row of teeth and claws. Did her mother leave the flashlight? You can hear a belly scoot over the scruffy gorse; it must be a lizard, or a tiny mouse; a hedgehog, a porcupine, an armadillo, an anteater, a tiger. In South America there are bats as big as people, they look like sacks of potatoes hanging upside down among the leaves; they wait for travelers to fall asleep, then after they've dozed off under the trees, the bats cover them with their large wings, and bend down; beneath these warm membranes, which hide the Moon, the traveler senses only the depths of sleep and night into which he lets himself sink, as his blood leaves him. She buries her head in the folds of the tent and the universe turns back into a big blue skirt stretched a little out of shape.

She takes off her shoes, shakes them, pours out the glistening grains. The humidity has made the sand stick together; her heels pull out clumps, cubes. The night is black and gashed with foam. The waves fall from high in the sky and the Moon tumbles in silvery glints that shear, crackling, through the shadows. If you stretched out your hand, straight ahead, you could just touch them with your fingertips. She takes a step back; lighthouses are screwed into the hinges of the sky. The sea is a vertical partition through which you need only to pass: water would slide from nose to cheeks, from chest to back, from belly to hips to buttocks—and flow together again; entering the sea would be like going through curtains. The sand gives way, deeply, with every step, ringing her ankles in a chill dampness; she will walk to the lighthouse, then on to the next one; when day comes she'll go to a café and sit outside, and in the evening she'll get a room with a view.

She can see the book bag on the rear window shelf in the car; her mother must have moved it. The phone card and her home number are underneath the flap, in case she ever gets lost. But this forest is larger, it seems, than all the forests she knows; they drove through it for a long time. She saw her face in the right side mirror (one eye, half a nose, and a close-up of her hand), and behind it that constant, fleeting, crazy-quilt impression of the forest: black and white flashes, streaming from the car as if from a lamp held high, cleaving space in long empty slices that banged against the windows, a thrumming of air. It has all faded; a nocturnal dishevelment grips the creaking, abandoned trees. Something sleeps in the forest, walks there, somnambulistic and as tall as the tree trunks. She climbs the dune; the sand caves into the fresh footprints. Now the tent is very small, almost invisible, blue on blue. The trunks crouch in the darkness. She's on an island; if she calls out, everything will awaken. A long white fold creases the sky. She feels herself slowly sluing round; set down on the dune and beneath the sky. The sea has invaded everywhere: black water has flowed into insect nests, craters in the sand, the furrows of roots, has drunk up footprints and forest, flooding the night. The air withdraws whenever the sea inhales, then returns, before the water swells again, taking up all the space, so that one cannot breathe except in small gulps, between two immense movements of the sea, between two tremors of the sky: by hiccuping, with streaming cheeks, and the oystery taste of seaweed on the tongue.

2

She was exactly the same as usual; she kissed the child, asked if everything had gone well. Everything had: she talked about school, coming back from school, snack time, the nature program on TV at five-thirty, homework. She was a bit late, as on evenings when she ran an errand beforehand. She was wearing her hair loose, which made her look youthful, almost childlike, plus, that sundress—had she worn it to work? A blue sundress, with straps crossed in the back. Perhaps it's the heat: you slip on a dress, one you wouldn't wear, normally, in town, and then you get ideas. Maybe they're at the movies. Or at a swimming pool open late at night, with fountains, slides, sprays of cool droplets. Opening the windows doesn't help—there's not a breath of air. She could have left a note, it's true. At one point, while the child was collecting her things (she didn't seem in a hurry, she was almost relaxed, letting the little girl take her own sweet time), she ran some water in the kitchen, you could hear it in the living room; when she went in five minutes later she was still there, leaning with both hands on the edge of the sink, bending over slightly, and the thought occurred to her: thin, too thin, the straps crossed over the sinuous spine as fragile as moss stitches knitted under the skin. Because it was one of those moments when, even if you reach out, you don't think you can touch the hologram standing in front of you (but pass through its listless body, perhaps, chivying its ghost with your fingers): she saw her there, deaf, blind, vulnerable, so sure she was alone that her body had gone limp, bearing down heavily on her wrists, shoulders high over cocked hips, backbone bent, ankles flexed to one side over sandals with heels, swaybacked, hanging suspended there, a woman grown, a stranger. She looks at the back, the crossed straps—it takes a second, the time to see her: the length of the bones, the buckled ankles, the place where the bleached color becomes darker roots; she reaches out, automatically, to turn off the faucet; the back shivers, the collarbones drop, the shoulder blades come together; the face turns, irritated in advance. She asks if the child is ready. Her cheeks are covered with a mist of droplets (she probably rinsed her face in her cupped hands) and a few tendrils of hair are sticking to her neck. As for her, she talks about the heat. About how the child was bathed in perspiration when she got out of school, about how there isn't adequate ventilation. But they're already gone. She stays there, in the empty apartment, in the shadowy stripes of the shutters. The net curtains barely stir, an illusion, a longing for coolness, unless a breeze sneaked into the apartment when they left and the afternoon is relaxing its grip at last. The shutters cast fluffy beams into the dim light, floating dust, luminous and oblique; if she stretches out her hand, or simply breathes a little deeply, she sees those fine filings of air, rubbed smooth against the furniture by the passing hours, begin to tremble; she feels—fleetingly—a draft return, doors opening, the square of light and the two shadows across the threshold. In southern Japan, in the humid heat of the summer, delicate bells are hung in the windows; from their clappers of bamboo, basalt, tin, or porcelain dangle fans: at the slightest puff, the pleated paper sweeps the bell along in a subtle song that eases the air. She crosses the living room, picks up the cups, a pencil left by the child; the curtains hang stiffly, sculpted in gauze. But if she stares at them, or if she looks just to the side, at the wall, as if playing a trick, she sees them sway, at the edge of her irises: the fine check pattern deepens, one window becomes two, white reflections flutter loose in folds, in curves, and the forms appear, shoulders raised, hips tilted, quivering gently with repressed energy. That's something she cannot tell her son-in-law: that she saw her, that she saw them, in the curtains, and in the doorway; that she often sees them, just after they've left, and occasionally at night. Of course it's the dust, iridescent in the sun between the shafts of shadow, weaving fingers, hair, hips. He's in front of her, she's not sure he's listening, he takes his head in his hands. He has already done everything necessary, the hospitals, the police stations, and now he's talking about consulting a detective. It's still too early yet, however; they might be at the movies, the last showing. It's a night that seems like the onset of summer. The heat has lifted, a little. She was the same as always, just exactly the same. She was staring at something in the sink. Her body was tense, crumpled, compact, crisply outlined against the light, yet at the same time suspended, from the collarbones, you might say, so that another body, more fluid, came loose and leaned forward, but shielded from the light, volatile and varying, blurred, out in front of the opaque body, kept connected to it only at the shoulders, by the crossed straps.

Do you have someone in mind? Someone she might have gone off to join? Eighty percent of the time, people consult him about adultery. Here, there's the kid, to complicate things. He sees a few cases of disappearance, a new life, a sea change, through the looking-glass: men, always; in debt, homicidal, in love, or worn out. You can't make them come back; you can make them pay up, sometimes. She'll do what they do. She'll make a mistake. Maybe she has already used a phone or credit card. He takes the photos. He puts them in his pocket with the check. The two men shake hands.

The people speak Spanish around here. They noticed this when buying fruit and some water. The border wasn't much more than a traffic circle and a blue flag with stars on it. When she turned back, the child woke up. The tight curve of the access road, the freeway again, going up and down, winding; purple mountains and fields full of darkness, trees with broad green leaves.

She'd been asleep until now. The sun beats down on the window. She sees herself in the rearview mirror: creased eyelids, squished hair, red nose, light shining through translucent nostrils and all the way in if she tips her head back. The air is already quite hot. Sand grains are rolling around under her T-shirt and itching her; ants, maybe. Her mother has stopped again. The seat of her new dress is wrinkled. Perhaps she bought it yesterday, right before she came to pick her up. She returns smelling of vanilla and hair spray; the old woman to whom she was speaking is still pointing off in one direction. The landscape passes all across the glass, the left window, the windshield, the right window: a river, the shade beneath the trees, rows of façades, and perhaps, behind, if one went on long enough, without any more U-turns, straight ahead, no stopping—the house, the market, the movie theater. Something of the grandmother now hovers in the car, with the hair spray and the vanilla, the way it does in the shuttered apartment when she goes there after school. Only because of the scratchy sand can she believe that she really spent the night on the dune, overlooking the sea and the woods—or rather, that this dream is among those that, when the sleeper awakes, leave behind (next to the bed, by the door, on the skin) a sign, a tattoo, a trace: the letter received in the nightmare, lying folded in quarters on the bedside table; the visitor's footprints; the broken pane of glass, where a scrap of his cape, a claw, a tuft of fur is caught; and perhaps, after the dream of the sea, the salty hair at daybreak, the anklets of seaweed. She'd like to have a bath. She's cold, in spite of the sun. In South America, explorers who have nodded off in the arms of vampires never lose the two tiny red dots on their necks: all their lives, no matter how much they rub, they'll carry the mark of their journey through the forests, and every evening, behind their eyelids, they'll see once more the tepid wings bending tenderly over their faces, solicitously shutting in the darkness. They'll be afraid to fall asleep.

The worst is the idea of the child during the night: Was she cold, was she scared? Light and dark mingle, entwine, collapse and rise again, like a flowing river, a road streaming by. When her son-in-law telephoned, early that morning, to say they still hadn't come home, she'd said nothing; she'd slipped on her bathrobe and closed both sets of curtains, making the room darker, setting the walls and furniture to turning, slowly. She should have kept them there, should have said something. With her son-in-law, yesterday, and this morning on the phone—the wish that he would be quiet or go away, since he would believe nothing of what she might say, since he would see nothing of the curtains moving, the water trickling from the tap, the shoulders beneath their straps, the shadows saturated with pollen. And he might accuse her of helping them run away. Outside cars brake or take off again; she hears children on the school path. A glimmer twinkles between the velvet curtains, setting airy tinder aflame. She feels the blood in her hand, in her wrist, in her arm up to her shoulder, she feels the arteries and veins, the red heat that overflows her lungs and then drains away in abrupt rushes; her heart beats too quickly, while a pain eats into her chest. The curtains flap, there's a spurt of light that vanishes, the glare throbs, swells, then ebbs, leaving sparks in the eyes and a tingling in the fingers. Her cheeks and eyes burn; drifting glassy spheres drag long bright tails behind them, they dive too deep, she's in the dark, she rises again, searching for air, a flash shatters the surface, fine white lines, far away, something that's now as big as the sky and that stops, there. She raises the curtain; the street is awash in daylight. There's a heartbreaking tree, a reminder that other trees exist and that simply strolling beneath their foliage would allow you to breathe again, to drink, tipping your head back, looking up at their clear and rippling water.

Sand has clumped in the tips of her sneakers: hard, gritty balls between her toes, that work patiently, meticulously, to pry off the nails. Hairy little tendrils have latched on to the laces, along with seeds, insect parts, burrs. Her mother blinks in the sunshine, studying the signs as they walk along the waterfront. She waits for her on a bench, kicks off her sneakers. She'd love to have the same shoes as the children here wear, she likes the exotic contrast between their backpacks (but surfers' backpacks, fluorescent with rainbow flaps) and their plastic sandals, soft as jelly. Her mother goes into some shops; the crossed straps of her sundress make two distinct dark lines behind the reflections on a store window, behind the children chasing one another, in the opaque whiteness of the sun. Birds fly by in the window, black, pointed, flapping like batting eyelashes. If she changes position slightly, she sees houses by swimming pools, palm trees, beaches, smiling families holding hands, a small boy on his father's shoulders, a dog sitting on his haunches: photos stuck behind the glass. Right next to the bench is a phone booth. The book bag was left in the car, a long way off, in another part of town. The dress in the window sways gently; the glass is glossy with sunlight. Shifting her line of sight, she watches this jutting angle become a hollow; that black shadow, a double white profile; this armchair, a crouching beast; that recess, an exit to the jetty. One sees, as if in a false bottom, a shimmering blue. She can imagine she's inside a big house, sitting in front of bay windows overlooking the sea: first, a blue that's very pale, then a dark line, and then more blue, darker, furrowed with white, gray, green, then a large blotch of turquoise that grows larger still.

Birds chirp: martins; the windowpane is full of swooping martins, gliding motionless the instant after the wing beat. They pepper the sun with little eclipses. You'd think there were brass pendulum bobs, springs that magnify the birds at the edge of the window lens, then snatch them in midair and gather them up in miniature, so that only the snow is missing, to shake up in a souvenir globe, a souvenir of a blue place where martins would fly. She lets the curtain fall back. The voices of the children outside, the noise of their chases on the crosswalk break into her brain, straining her skull at the sutures. Her chest still hurts; she goes to lie down and wait.

A simple wrist movement, the steering wheel turning this way instead of that, the changing landscape, the kid silent with surprise, uneasiness, and the scenery persisting stubbornly and marvelously (or even: without your realizing it) in its strangeness—he understands all that, and the kind of emptiness of those alterations, which one must drive past, reject, going farther, until one finds something truly empty, completely new. The client refuses to believe you cannot find everything (evidence of a purchase, the rental of a hotel room, passage through tollbooths), cannot eavesdrop on their conversations via satellite, track their heartbeats. He spends the morning and evening at the agency. He plans to have their pictures circulated by the press, in stations, at freeway service areas. He's just amazed by the porosity of borders, by the indifference of space, of roads, by their continuity, by the breadth of continents, by the vastness of the sea. As for the client, he listens to him, it's part of the job. He tries to repress the reflexes of anguish: posters, the purchase of a weapon, the occupation of a police station, a hunger strike. As for the rest, one must be patient.

She still hasn't used her bank card. She's paying for everything in cash, having emptied the joint account before leaving, ten thousand francs. Soon she'll be forced to find something else. If she hasn't left the country, she might feel she should register the kid in school, but it's coming up on the end of May, and even supposing she tries this, they might make her wait until September. He fixes himself some coffee, looks at the photos again. To put oneself there, behind those eyes, behind that forehead; to lift up that hair, to seize the thoughts beneath the smooth surface; to see the roads, the trees, the places, the people. He would go meet her, show her his card; he'd tell her they've been looking for her, and how many days the investigation has been going on. She'd open her eyes wide, brush back her hair. It would be sunny, as in the photograph, and he would have to lean over, move forward to see her. The lens has cast a bright reflection upon her face, three circles of decreasing size, edged with white around a rainbow center, three circles that—if you stop to consider them—are stars blurred by their own light. One of these circles has landed on an eye, decapsulating the iris, and if you really look, if you block the brain's automatism for a moment, the compensation it provides for a woman's face (routinely filling in the eyes, nose, mouth, and the appropriate form), then you see this face, almost one-eyed, a blind spot on the right iris, the other strangely displaced by a lock of hair whose movement, at this angle, has been flattened against the middle of her forehead—and that sun-splash, scoring the eyelid but seaming the nose as well, with a last round flash falling at the corner of the lips, cutting short the hem of the smile, so that the mouth has been left lopsided, unfinished.

Great chunks of cliff lie on the beach, lined up in the order of their collapse; grass and trees still grow on them, pieces of the gardens above, diced into cubes showing, in a geological cross section, the thin layer of green lawn, then the tangle of roots, then sandy clay— ocher, wormholed by runoff water—and lastly the grainy bottom, the whole snapped off as cleanly as a broken piece of pottery. All askew, a tamarisk shades the waves; the soil has crumbled away from its roots as big as branches, stretching emptily toward the salt water, writhing in vegetal horror. She looks up; there remains, where the cliff has sheared off, a hollow impression, a negative of what has fallen, the outline of a cavity that is mottled and smooth, as if the earth had contracted so as not to slip anymore; and just above, the ruins of some rotunda, greenhouse, orangery, or winter garden (people were dancing, drinking— painters, aviators, crooks with leather steamer trunks, White Russians, their noses stuffed with cocaine), a section of colonnade, part of a leaded glass window, shattered azulejos, and then foundations around blocks of air, gutted cellars, subbasements plunging into pits, and deeper still, toward the beach, long, naked rods, the roots of reinforced concrete. If a body had been concealed there, it would have tumbled down with the cliff, mummified, sitting exposed in the shadow of the phantom tamarisk. The child is looking elsewhere, someplace vague, perhaps where the town meets the sea, toward the mountains growing hazy with heat. She really should buy her an ice cream cone.

The sea has emptied one entire side of the landscape. To the left there are red and white houses, deserted cafés, an ice cream vendor, and then the pale curve of the mountains; to the right, as if the earth had sunk for lack of beach, there is only the sea, absent, blue, motionless under a glaze of radiance. The children in plastic sandals have disappeared; a few old ladies stroll idly along, preceded by perfectly straight leashes and little dogs up on their hind legs, their noses blue with asphyxia. She'd like to go back now. Her sneakers methodically scrape the soles of her feet with each step. They're heading toward the ice cream man. In front of the colored tubs, heart pounding, she strains to read the labels. Her heels are getting hot. The hand holding hers is squeezing harder, she must choose, she can have two scoops, so she picks at random: brown for chocolate, and then pink—strawberry, that's safe. The scoop plunges in, clacking, scattering white flickers, drops of light. Her tongue brings back, unavoidable, the disgusting flavor of praline. She doesn't dare taste the other scoop, the pink one, that trickles slowly down the cone; she doesn't know anymore what to do with the big hollow in her chest, the ants eating up her heels, the greedy tension that climbs her calves to take up all the space, there, along the waterfront, dismembering the sky, the sea, the cliff, and the town shaped like a flight of stairs.

3

She's pleased to have found something so quickly. She'll have to turn in the keys at the beginning of July, when the seasonal rentals begin, but she can return in mid-September, if she wants. The agency displays pictures of houses that look like vacation memories. Through the plate-glass window, she sees the waves, the beach, the ice cream man out in sunshine that is already growing warm. The city is as hollow as a seashell, coiled up in the curls of the cliff. Here rentals are by the week in summer; the seaside is like that. In the summertime, the real estate agent tells her, the population increases tenfold, and you should have seen the ocean before the new water-treatment plant, for sewage, you understand. She sees the summer, the haze of heat on the mountains, the windows swimming with blue reflections, the yellow light filling the city. The still air that gels like a mousse and grows hotter, flattening the sea, drawing the horizon closer, compressing the summer to the melting point. She sees the surfers, who pull the waves after them, a breath of cool air on the sand, and the children darting out from under the beach umbrellas, shouting in the white silence draped over the sunbathers like a sheet. She signs the papers. It's next door, a few yards to the left, a lobby with a tiled floor. With the keys she receives a complimentary kit containing packets of instant coffee, a small box of detergent, and some samples of sunblock lotion. The samples have the same drawing of a house and family as the agency photos.

They leave; he watches them through the front window. The little girl looks like a miniature of her mother. They have the pale, slender bodies of visitors, the thin white arms, the ankles that look ready to snap. The faint wash of the sea this morning is more than enough to erase the noise of their footsteps. Their faces make a bright mark, a nimbus that sails across the store windows amid glints from the sea, the cars, the wristwatches of passersby. An ice cream's violent pink dribbles over the child's fingers, a stain chest-high and growing ever larger, gleaming in the sunlight. Perhaps they're traveling. The father is in the harbor, on a sailboat. There are some like that, every year, going around the world, who stop over to find work, leave again three months later. While they're in town, they read to the children. They surf, drive around in vans, sail from place to place looking for waves: California, Hawaii, Australia, and they always wind up passing through here.

Today the sea isn't up to much. It heaves carelessly, sinks back without any effort, an elastic arterial pulsation; two hours from now will be low tide, at noon, with the sun at its zenith, and then everything will start all over again, the tide rising toward the old harbor, toward the casino, toward the blue store window. At seven o'clock, when he lowers the curtain, it will be high tide. He'll feel it behind him, close, peaceful, immense. He'll go home along the cliff, you can see farther, breathe more freely. Now they're turning toward the lobby; he cranes his neck. She nods slightly to him. Their hair melts in the light, a ray of sun has fallen on them, dissolving them; in their wake they leave wisps of hair that glow and are gone. Now they must be in the elevator that dispenses a synthetic strawberry antitobacco scent every time its doors open; they reach the twelfth floor of the huge building, ugly and already old, that brought down the mayor and destroyed the seafront but has a lovely view. It's a place for her: he explained that to her, within the limits of the discretion inherent in his profession, in the idea he has of his profession. For a single woman, for two people, or more (a studio, what does that mean? Sailboats that go around the world aren't any bigger), it's a place where you can have peace and quiet, gaze out over the sea, and feel right away that you're on vacation. It's fully furnished. He lives on the thirteenth floor, the highest floor, and has a small balcony overlooking the top of the cliff: the building was constructed—that was the original pretext—to strengthen the cliff on one side. When you look at the map, it is, in the event of a tidal wave, a safe place, one the sea cannot touch. Or else you have to run, to the first foothills of the mountains. She shook his hand rather quickly when he tried to elaborate on his approach to the concept of accommodation. He'd like to write a book on the subject; for writing, a seascape is ideal. But all she cared about was the view. It's their desire for the view that motivates most clients.

The glass in the windows is so transparent that before opening them, she hesitates, just for a moment, long enough to notice the almost invisible marks of raindrops, their mineral ghosts, or perhaps the salty traces of spindrift. She leans out; the sun hasn't reached them yet, they're obviously facing west, full western exposure overlooking the sea, so only the sharp bend in the cliff, where the Art Deco houses are collapsing, is getting any sun. It's hard to know where to look, how to decide: what's ending, what's beginning—the full side or the empty one; which piece of the planet borders the other, the blue subsidence of the sea, or the furnished heights of the city; whether the coast has given way before the waves, or the waves have found a berth, an anchorage here, as if the ocean's mass were

holding on to the earth with only the wavering, weak-
ened, renewed grip of its edge of lacy foam. The little
girl hasn't finished her cone, she's covered with
dribbles, it's always the same with ice cream. She
sponges the child off over the sink, gives her a glass of
water, then lets the water run until it's hot enough to
make instant coffee. The unbreakable cups and glasses
are decorated with the same seagull as the bedspreads.
She pulls a chair over to the window; the sea clings to
the beach, covering the sandy floor, the wrecks, the
dead cities, and lingers on, settled and amnesic: a
smooth blue mirror, so smooth and so blue that it's
hard to believe in its depths, a shield burnished by a
buffing wheel and curved at the periphery, delicately
embossed with a hammer. Swimming ten strokes out
from the shore, however, you would hover above the
void, suspended, confident, thinking you could still
just touch bottom, even though your body, seen from
below, would no longer be anything more than a pale
specter outlined against a murky light, like the bell of
a submerged church tower. There must be creatures
down there, the child has to have seen those nature
programs, she knows all about that kind of thing: fa-
mous shipwrecks, whales like cathedrals under the sea,
sharks that confuse surfers with seals (the surfboard is
the body, the hands and feet are the flippers, and bang,

the water bleeds in the sunshine, and the boards are found chomped on like apples).

She plays with the laces of her sneakers, making one bow, then another, then undoing them and starting over. Her blisters have gone down. The wind comes softly through the window, a light morning breeze that ruffles the downy hairs at her temples. They've been living in that apartment four days now. First they go buy an ice cream, then they sit outside the pâtisserie; her mother orders coffee, she drinks a glass of milk. They stay there for a long time. Schoolchildren go home for lunch; the owner of the pâtisserie lowers the awning against the sun. In the afternoon they walk along the shore. She's enrolled in the Blue Dolphins Club, which opens at 4 p.m., and as early as 10 a.m. on Wednesdays. In the evening they eat at the apartment—pasta, cheese, and fruit—in the waning light that casts deep shadows around their eyes. Her mother chats, from balcony to balcony, with the man from the agency. At the end of the hall, beneath the sheets on the top bunk, she hears the zigzag of voices in the red night sky. They talk about the sea, the present calm and the workings of the Moon, the swell expected at the solstice (when the Earth tilts suddenly on its axis, big waves come rolling in), the approaching surfing championships, and the tourists who are beginning to arrive; her mother's voice becomes porous, purple, shot through with the sun's last rays; the words slow down, stretch out, coil up; she no longer hears the man's voice, she sees the ocean and the surfers, the ice cream man in his little truck, the cliff smoking in the white light. She nestles beneath the worn sheets, clasping the pillow in her arms. With one eye she can make out her mother, leaning on her elbows, her back and neck slightly twisted as she speaks to the terrace above. The hem of her dress hangs down around her ankles, and the light—a low, raking light—catches in the fabric: the material becomes violet, almost black, dotted with burning holes. The shoulder straps have disappeared in darkness. To all appearances, a tall triangular body with two arms and a head emerging from membranous flesh, floating in the breeze, a body with that voice, distant, detached, like a reply to words long gone: a hollow voice, vesperal. She feels her mother's hands in her hair: she's lying with her face buried in her lap. She's not crying anymore. The sand gleams, the pines creak, the dune devours the forest; she hears that voice, back again, a deep voice that comes not from the throat but from the belly, she hears it through her nose, her eyes, her mouth, a voice that fills out the whole body and wraps big nocturnal arms around her. She turns over, moves the sheet slightly aside; with her back to the night, her mother is looking at her. She instantly closes her eyes; she hears the rest of the sentence, a

ripple in the phrase, a quick swerve: her father, whis-
pers her mother, has gone off on a trip. She thinks
about the night, which will turn black; about the blue
reflection the sea would throw off if she managed to
escape, to find her book bag, to telephone.

She sold the car to a garage owner in a seaside resort—
the record of her car registration has given her away.
The client agrees to pay him an advance; he hangs up,
opens an atlas. On the two-page spread of the planisphere, the sea is not that enormous, but it ends and
begins everywhere. How does one decide that the seashore is *here*? Does one forget about boats, planes?
Bodies stand out against the continents: animals, monsters, some of those brawny horned beasts with the
heaviness of fossils wrenched from the clay, stubborn,
brutish, brow and muzzle butted up against the land.
The Atlantic is an elephant, its trunk wound around
Cuba, its tusks curved beneath Iceland. The Indian
Ocean is a two-horned rhinoceros straining against
Africa; from a certain angle, it's also an ancient camel,
its humps flanking India. It takes some effort (the
map is centered on Europe) to see the Pacific, to piece
it back together, rearing up against the Earth: it's a
bison, a yak, a buffalo, tall in the withers; it gores
China, tramples Tasmania, kicks at Tierra del Fuego.

The paradox is that the continents are seals, whales, and manatees. He's known that since he was a boy. He trained himself early on to see the reverse of the planisphere; it's a healthy exercise, almost an ascesis, toning the optic nerves, the arteries and muscles; the abdominals grow taut, the genitals retract; you must forget cities, plains, valleys, and look at gulfs as projections, harbors as bridgeheads, breakers as the end of the world, and islands as abysses: then you see the blue, the shape of the blue. He closes the atlas, has a good stretch. He'll be going someplace where there are waves. He'll rent a small apartment and smoke out on his balcony. In the evening he'll stroll around, read the paper outside a café, greet the regulars. He'll learn the tide tables and which seasons are the best for fishing, he'll know the names of dangerous channels. He'll have an opinion on drift nets, on the demarcation of territorial waters. Reading the newspaper, he'll pay particular attention to the weather.

A few rare cars go by. It's three o'clock. The traffic light changes, imperturbable. The downstairs door latch buzzes. Her skirt is wrinkled, her hairdo is sticking to her temples and has lost some of its curl around her neck. The sun keeps battering the walls; the concrete makes a blinding gash in the lime bath smoking against the sky. Her son-in-law woke her up with the name of a seaside resort town. To see the ocean—

nothing could be easier; to see the ocean, to hear it in a seashell. On this point, only some illness, or gross insensitivity, can paralyze the senses: the sky breaking up, the horizon, the clouds, and the tremendous expanse enlarging the view to encompass the world. She knows that city's name, everyone does; a city of vacations, waves and swimming pools, trees, and villas glimpsed only as a section of wall, a red-and-white breach in the blue. She has seen reports on TV, received postcards, heard stories (Basques play pelota, sport berets, have O− blood and no earlobes, their language was spoken by the inhabitants of Atlantis, and they still bear the scars, below the mastoid, of what once were gills). She bends down, massages her legs, rolling the hard balls of varicose veins beneath her skin. She closes her eyes; she longs constantly to sleep. Dreams bring her something of the child, a kind of sparkle, a color, a way of imprinting the air, of altering the places where she's been. She would like to be sure she isn't muddling things—memories would be out of place. It's her face that appears, a broad, pale halo, beaming, then stern, the mouth, nose, smaller and smaller, she hasn't time enough to see, the city reclaims her, as if she were seen through the portholes of a rocket taking off: the ground falling away, the periphery expanding as it empties out, things sinking in the center, dropping into the funnel of the center, until they come out again (we're led to believe) on the other side—the red-and-white houses, the roofs that fold back, the streets that roll themselves up, the cliff that rises and rewraps the beach, and the sea, even more vast and blue, overflowing into the city, into the sky; you pass through a curtain of clouds and the city disappears in mist, a great plain of white vapor, beyond which emerge, like a photo from silver salts, lines, coasts, no longer waterfronts but a geography, gulfs, mountains, the spectacular curve of the Atlantic's shores. The sea has taken all the space, the coasts have moved apart, they are moving still (the plates slide, the oceanic rift tears America from Europe, nodules shoot forth to the rhythm of black submarine vents, ruining undersea Pompeiis and the devices of Captain Cousteau), and her room turns blue, with two little skullcaps on the poles and a scattering of continents.

She opens her eyes; the apartment is silent, dead of sunstroke. She feels her forehead, her cheekbones: her face is puffy from the heat or sleepiness, a blur of marks on the windowpane. Cars drive over her cheeks and her forehead is pierced by the windows across the street. The sun shimmers; dazzling flashes of light set things ablaze and obliterate them. The latticed balcony delicately divides the air into squares, and quivers. She gives up trying to sort out what she sees; otherwise, everything giving way inside will completely overwhelm her.

The latticework keeps shifting position: drawing near, out of focus in the foreground, with disproportionately huge squares; or on the contrary, slipping into the depths of the landscape, so that now the tree, the houses, the street, and the traffic light come closer, gigantic, with hazy outlines, sieved into millions of little cubes. The two visions, front and back, reverse themselves, swap places; edges jut out or cave in, the perspective turns around. Watching science programs on TV—the life of atoms, anatomy, plate tectonics—she and the child were endlessly intrigued by that kind of difference: the two sides of the same world, the magma that lifts up the laths of the planet, flowing like a serum, organic, astounding, but most of the time invisible and hidden underground, beneath familiar blacktop, streets, school playgrounds, public squares, parking lots. The little girl's astonishment at all this—she would like it to go on and on, to last like the perpetual flux of things, she'd like to continue fostering it, for as long as possible, and whatever hasn't yet collapsed in her brain warns her that she must leave right away.

She's learning to swim in the Blue Dolphins Club. The instructor's name is Patrick. First you stick your head in the water, and you blow out with your mouth while

counting to three. Then you hold on to the ladder at
the edge, you float on your tummy, and kick your feet;
finally you hang on to a long pole and let yourself be
pulled along, puffing like a sea lion. This happens at
the pool. You cross the waterfront and the casino
porch and go down some stairs. It's very hot; steam
with a musty smell of chlorine wells up like strong foot
odor. The two other children learning to swim are
Steve and Maïté. They leave their book bags in the
locker room and eat snacks wrapped in aluminum foil.
The locker-room floor feels damp underfoot; big cold
drops fall from the ceiling. An iron bar always seems to
be banging against pipes or in the basements, each
handle turned on the lockers clatters like forty metal
doors, and voices sound as though they were echoing
off armor plating, with yells and shrieks ringing
sharply in the muggy air. She feels woozy from the taste
of the water. It's salty. Maïté is crying, she says it makes
her eyes sting. Steve says a pipe goes under the casino,
pumping seawater, sometimes sucking up a shark, and
when it's the other way round, when the pool is emptied, they risk getting swept away to the bottom of a
big trough inhabited by transparent fish. She ducks her
head under; the water grips her hair and noises fill her
brain. You sputter air, the outside world is a clatter of
bubbles in the water; once you get used to it, you hear
the forge beneath the cavern, the creaking of unseen

chariots, the scraping metal of moving limbs and the crash of divers: the pool gives way, then flows together again, slowly, behind the body that emerges, smooth and glossy. When she has run out of air, she raises her head, and it's like a memory coming back to her: the matte quality of things, Patrick's clear voice, the cries that scatter cleanly between the vault and the splashing. Water is a great rest, a hand held out beneath the body. You don't have to beware of the ground anymore, keeping it at a distance, remembering your muscles and straightening your spine. You don't have to watch out, to stay awake. Water resembles sleep. She no longer hears Maïté's sobs, or people's shouts, or Steve's stories. She lets go of the edge, swims in forgetfulness of the water, head submerged, body in motion and newly supple. When Patrick lifts her up at the end of the pole, she has grown the curves of a carapace, and continues her rock-lobster siesta at the end of her fisherman's arm. Her mother helps her slip on her sweater, moving aside lobster legs, folding back antennae as she talks to Patrick. They linger at the exit. She tries to hear what they're saying.

He hopes that with the money from the car, she hasn't taken to the skies as well, the both of them crossing paths, separated by air, the fuselage, emptiness. He's in economy class, wondering how much he should charge his client. The plane is deserted. The flight attendants are standing in the aisle, chatting. The din from the jet engines is so loud, in the rear, that he gives up trying to ask for another seat and lets the noise wash through him. The clouds have strange shapes, whites he's never seen before; the plane flies around them without leaving a whirl or a wrinkle in their suspended mass, as if a total silence on the other side of the window had made the vapor congeal. Frozen avalanches hang over the wings. Sculpting a gaseous geography, fortuitous in its freeze-frame, the air gilds the tops of the clouds; a delicate orange shadow holds them as if in the hollow of a hand. He shouts for someone to bring him a whiskey. The attendant shows him how to use the call button. The clouds have vanished. He twists around in his seat, trying to glimpse, in the corner of the window, a last vertical slab of whiteness; he sees only his face, layered by the triple-paned window. His eyes have an expression he hadn't known, that he wouldn't recognize in a photo, supposing that photos of such fugues exist: an expression that eludes his flesh and that he could not control from behind his face, a loss of mastery so complete—even though fleeting, stemming from memories of climax or childhood—that he hopes no one caught sight of his reflection. The attendant takes the glass from his hand, gently puts up the seat back

and tray table, and motions to him, with a patient
smile, to fasten his seat belt. For a second he fears she'll
tuck a blanket around his legs; there's a faint odor of
mint and the sanatorium about the plane. We have
begun our descent, the pilot announces to the empty
cabin, and we wish you a pleasant weekend. The coast
is bright yellow alongside the green sea.

She has completely forgotten the book bag, it's gone,
with the car. The child is still open-mouthed after her
question, her eyes made ugly by an unpleasant fear. She
would like to tell her that it's only a book bag, that
they'll buy another. She touches the money in her
pocket, the crackling thickness of new bills, a contact
that is extremely beneficial. She looks for words, even
one, to share this tranquillity with her, to invite her to
look at the scenery, the beauty of sunlight on the sea,
the surfers riding the swell of the solstice. She hesitates,
taps on the table between the coffee and the glass of
milk. Now the child is going to cry; before she honks
her little foghorn, she ought to take her on her lap,
with hugs and promises, holding her so tightly she'd
understand with relief where that small portion of
space they must inhabit begins and ends. She places her
hand on the child's; she feels, beneath her palm, a
young rabbit sweating and trembling with a motion-

less reticence, muscular and tetanized. She stands up to pay the bill, blinks, and the sunny sea clouds over like a sky. It's a flight of black spots, as fleeting as a dizzy spell. She thought, in the forest, that she'd lost her. She was only going to look at the sea, climb the dune and look at the sea. She returned; the tent was empty. Branches sliced through the darkness. The forest surrounded her. The sand fell away in shadow, quickly, beneath her steps. And then she saw her, an elf, through the black boles. She caught her, that fragile little body ready to melt in the night air, to dissolve in the surge of the forest; thought of swallowing her, reclaiming her; making her go back inside her womb, placing her arms inside her arms, her belly inside her belly, her head inside her skull. She leans for an instant on the back of the chair. The squeak of a pipistrelle fades from her hearing, sunshine returns to the sea and the cliff, the shadows retreat into their caves. The water rustles, twinkling with silver, green, and gold as far as the eye can see. She is stretched out under a tall poplar; she is in the upside-down trees. A plane passes, tracing a white line where the sky is. It dips toward the earth, it's about to land, the jet engines engulf the sound of the waves.

Her eyes follow the shadowy cross gliding over the sea. She slept through most of the flight, it was the pilot's voice that awakened her. Quickly she asks for another glass of champagne. She hasn't taken enough advantage of her first-class seat; she stretches her legs, massages them, rubs her burning face with some graciously offered eau de cologne. If she'd dared, she could have lain down across the whole row of seats. The flight attendant has opened the curtains; the airplane is almost empty. A postcard gleams below the window: a yellow beach, a white casino, a red luxury hotel; you can make out rows of cabanas; the sea cuts notches, scooping out streets with two-toned façades. She would have to stay like this, in the air, with her forehead pressed against the window, and lift up every roof, shake every car, tip over every cabana, and she would find them, she'd pluck them up between two fingers. The sea is green, flat, hammered like a sheet of copper; in the plane's shadow you can see through to the bottom, a long fish of seaweed and rocks, skimming over blue sands. The champagne is giving her a headache. She's got the hiccups, she opens the airsickness bag but manages only to cough. The plane banks; blood leaves her legs to come pound in her head.

Puffs of humid air have entered the aircraft, bringing a peaceful, salty warmth. The flood of noise from the jet engines subsides. He grabs his carry-on suitcase. The flight attendants in their blue caps say goodbye. He waits at the top of the passenger steps—in the wind, it's like a scene from a movie—while a steward finishes helping a red-faced old woman. You have to disembark right on the tarmac and walk over to the airport. He's as happy as a child. Some rabbits are sitting at a distance, hypnotized by the activity. Golfers keep a weather eye open at the far end of the runway, mowing the sky with long swings borne aloft by the foehn.

4

He lowers the metal shutter, and the sun goes down with a grating sound; the white paint is flaking off, he'll have to look into all that. He puts on his dark glasses, takes a few steps back. His name is still clearly visible, dark gray in the lambent light. You have to try, every now and then, to see with new eyes. That's what he explains to his clients, so proud, most of them, of the house they're putting on the market. The buyer, he tells them, will notice the cracks, the roughcast chewed up by the sand, the dribbles of rust on the ironwork, the shutters pitted by the termites of the salt air; especially the buyers of inland property, who come here to retire: those people fear the effects of the sea with a blinding terror. No one takes him seriously until a few months have gone by and the FOR SALE sign on the weather-beaten façade is beginning to peel as well.

With the temperature rising, every evening he gets a craving for ice cream. Cormorants dynamite the sea, each dive exploding a grenade of coolness on the metallic surface. He chats with Lopez, who has made improvements: now he offers syrups, coatings, you dip

the ice cream and it comes out enrobed in chocolate,
you sprinkle on almonds or coconut, people like that.
The wind from the south clatters against the booth and
stings the cheeks, bringing a smell of oasis; the Sahara
comes up here in gusts, blasts of nomadic sand; tomorrow the awnings, door frames, doorsteps will be ocher
from this African dust. He hesitates for a long time
before choosing his topping. Lopez shows him how
to twirl the ice cream in its cone, and the chocolate
hardens instantly. Just as he's about to decide on the
coconut, he senses their presence, the child and her
mother, in front of the tubs. He'd like to say something
witty, ask the ladies what they're having, but Lopez
has beaten him to it, he knows that the child wants
chocolate-strawberry, and the lady, nothing. He takes
a thoughtful bite; later he will realize that neither
the ice cream nor the coating left any taste in his
memory. The little girl's hair is full of sand, the downy
strands around her forehead have stuck together in
tiny clumps. As for her, she's still wearing her dress;
never pants, never a sweater. He suspects she washes
her things every evening for the next day. The weather
is on her side: an even temperature, mild, low humidity, thanks to the foehn. Her hipbones show beneath
the blue fabric, stretching it across her stomach; the
pleats drop smoothly in straight, deep folds that cover
her ankles in shadow. She turns slightly away; the

espadrilles point toward the sea, the knee creates a new fold, and the thigh, in the southerly wind, attracts a clinging panel of cloth. He sees himself taking a step and feeling, almost absentmindedly, the tip of her hipbone thrust against him. The child has called out. Her plastic sandals make a sound like suction cups on the paving stones of the waterfront. It's the guy from the beach club. He would now like, urgently, to get rid of his ice cream cone. The black neoprene of the wet suit encircles impeccably slender ankles; he's barefoot, and towers over them all by a head; he kisses mother and daughter on both cheeks. As for him, he shakes her hand, they say a few words about the influx of vacationers. Lopez is thrilled with the temperature, between 78 and 82 degrees, if it could just keep on like that, above 86 people stop eating ice cream. They look for explanations. His cone melts stickily over his fingers, which suddenly feel like wiping themselves on the dress that billows gently a few inches away. A strange calm has slowed the waves; voices cease; the sea falls silent. Light—a sunbeam—flashes across the child's face; he turns his head, he sees the section break loose, 500 yards away, he feels the bodies move closer together, the space among them set like plaster, from that one collapse, that one movement throughout the city: the cliff letting slip an immense vertical slab. The massive blocks sink into the sand without any explosion or spray of debris; it's after they've landed that they break up under their own weight, pieces shearing off suddenly, geometrical and yellow, leaving their edges sharp and new. Startled bats have swarmed out, catching fire in the sun. Then the sound rumbles, alien, penetrating.

The sea starts up again, and the cars; the taxi driver whistles admiringly as he drives on. A friend of his, who fishes down there, says that first you hear a gunshot, that's the section pulling away; it has already fallen while you're seeing it still up there, held in place by the sound lag, and surprise. The chunk of cliff has left a gleaming golden gash in the living rock. He didn't see a thing. He was idly looking at the gutted houses, three columns on the edge of the drop, split by pins and open fractures; the columns are still there, it's a remaining section of garden that went. The beach is strewn with hydrangea petals, the aftermath of a party, swept away by waves. He asks the driver if he may smoke, pulls the photo from his pocket. He plasters her to the window, where she passes by the houses, the beach, the waterfront, climbs a winding route up the flank of the cliff. The bubbles of sunlight follow her. He questions the driver; no, he doesn't know her. His hotel room has a view of the sea, which he isn't obliged to tell the client, and anyway it's a good observation post. On the right is the lighthouse; on the left, the city.

Just below, buttressing the cliff along with other modern buildings, a big, white, metallic hotel rigged out with terraces and awnings is breathing with a noise like machinery. He wonders where she lives, and if she's thinking about the future.

To study the brown bears of the Canadian steppe, scientists mark out a perimeter, not necessarily a very large one, and walk. The only danger, in these zones near the ice pack, is stumbling across a wide-awake polar bear. The brown bears, however, hibernate beneath the snow. So the scientists walk, in a line, that's the army's method for finding bodies. Someone finally feels, beneath his boot soles, snow that is softer, looser, snow that has been disturbed. Digging with his gloves, he uncovers a few chewed-on branches, beneath which snores black fur. The bear receives an injection to put it into a slightly deeper sleep; it barely twitches, a bee has stung it, up on a hive, it's gorging on honey, its adorable chops are quivering with pleasure. Then they study it, weigh it, stretch it out, tattoo it, they judge by touch its extraordinary powers of retention, they draw blood, analyze its tears, peer at its pensive eye. Certain sentimental researchers suggest a name; it's baptized, pawed over. The unique gentleness of this contact is hard to give up; they all want to take it in their arms to put it back in its den. Now comes the most delicate part: the drying. All this handling has introduced snow under fur that is normally waterproof, so the sleeping bear risks catching pneumonia. The scientists have ordered little portable battery-powered hairdryers from Whirlpool. They form a circle around the bear in the buzzing of its dream beehive. The bear's fur steams, curls; now they put back the snow, with a happiness in their faces that is almost painful to see.

There's a knock on the door; it's the doctor, in his white coat with the striped monogram of the thalassotherapy clinic. He listens to her chest, palpates her abdomen. The scientists get back on their snowmobiles and the sky grows dark over the steppe, as slanting rays of violet light skim crests of snow tinted orange. Rest is what you need, your pressure's a little low; did you see the cliff collapse? He's scribbling down a program of care providing for vitamin-enriched meals and vitalizing massages. The diet of the Galápagos sea turtle is difficult to determine; the feces are passed in the water, dissolving irretrievably in the sea. He takes the remote control from her hands, lowers the volume. It's the south wind that brings on headaches; your energy will return with exercise, I'm giving you this to help you sleep. A Franco-American team came up with the idea of attaching condoms to the turtles' shells to recover the excreta; the animals were hauled on board, she strains to hear the rest, they look like blocks of stone, with enormous fossilized eyes, and that's when the discovery was made (science advances crabwise, Fleming was studying molds when he stumbled across penicillin) that seawater dissolves latex. The big, passive monsters dance in the turquoise water with the elegance of manta rays—then we cut boldly to bits of latex decomposing in greenish test tubes. The doctor has gone, leaving some complimentary chocolates in striped wrappers. Chewing, she supports herself against the wall as she goes out to the balcony. Now *there's* the answer to the problems of sea pollution, the supermarket bags (currently of plastic) getting stuck in propellers, cluttering up fishing nets, blocking the intestines of marine mammals, and panicking moray eels into slicing one another to ribbons. The sound of the TV reaches her intermittently, drowned out by the sea. The wind has fallen. The city is disintegrating in the sun. A dense mist is rising, the air is burning itself up, the sea and the walls are evaporating. The awnings of the thalassotherapy clinic ripple limply, stripes above and below her grow taut, sag, and the building flaps like a becalmed sailboat. A yellow smear marks the spot where the cliff gave way; she'd had just time enough, while the luggage was being taken care of, to perceive a general movement of collapse, as though the city were subsiding around the break. The receptionists behind their counter, the bellboys, the porters, the elevator operators, all froze, then exploded into avid commentary, while she—she remained facing the luggage, on the margin of what was happening. She is lying in a deck chair; she needed a blanket, in spite of the sunshine. Extra cushions were brought to her, and an herbal tea with trace elements. Tomorrow, as soon as possible, when she feels better, she will begin looking for them.

The weather is changing. The haze remains, suspended, blurring the mountains, pushing them back to the far edge of the landscape, barely a mauve line halfway up a sky of blotting-paper blue. The landscape has expanded, the air is swelling, the sea is rising, not in waves, but by a kind of internal depression, as if through the suction of an octopus backed up against the continent, in the troughs where the ocean begins. The Moon has such effects; on a very large scale (that of the hemispheres), you can observe, via satellite, the formation of a basin, a veritable crater: it's the Moon driving away the water, fooling the forces of gravity, crushing the ocean in its center and raising the tide (a physical phenomenon easy to observe: press in the center of an unbaked tart crust, and the dough will climb up the sides of the pan). Then the Moon catches its breath, inhales the atmosphere: the depression turns inside out and into a hummock, a cone, as the sea withdraws from its shores. At the times of greatest effect, equinox and solstice, the crater or the cone is so pronounced, each in turn, that the beaches are bared to the quick, long-forgotten boulders emerge, limpets are asphyxiated, and anemones dry out, until the tide floods in once again.

She ponders the stories Patrick tells her at the pool, wonders about the Great Siphon, spinning in the center of the sea when the planet tilts on its axis, revolving in one direction or the other, depending on whether you're north or south of the equator. This evening, while brushing her teeth, she pulled out the drain plug to watch the little whirlpool; Patrick says that in Australia, where he plans to emigrate soon, the water flows in the opposite direction (and the Moon shines upside down). Before her mother sent her off to bed she saw the weather map on TV, those big curled-up masses whirring away at the slopes of the Earth. She awakened to a dark and windy night. The door slams shut between the studio and the corridor with the benches. Something like a residue of sun remains, red and scattered under the black sky. The apartment is empty. There's light on the thirteenth floor, in the neighbor's place. The fluorescent sea seems to have absorbed the day's energy to melt it into shining, lacquered waves.

The sea rises and falls, slowly, without haste, strong in its mass, full of octopuses, whales, hurricanes, ship-wrecks, bestowing on the city the edge of its presence. It makes her feel grown-up to be here, alone on the seashore; to stay here, at the precise place where land and sea come together. She's sitting in the chair her mother usually occupies; it's right next to the window, the balcony is too narrow. She's watching, waiting, she'd like to hear the voices. The studio glows faintly; the bed, the cupboard, the glasses left on the table seem softly lustrous, as if during her walks she had herself become so charged with sun that she now sufficed, like the sea, to shed her own light on the world. She tried to trace, on the weather map, the journey they had taken; she can recognize the place: at the bottom, to the left, in the curve, on the straight line of beaches, as easy to draw as a tightrope walker's wire. You balance there on one foot like a heron; past the waterfront, you're already quite far from the delicate outline of the waves and it's hard to find the capital, inland, somewhere in the middle. She sees the apartment, the apartment where they live. On this side, the door to her parents' bedroom. On the other, the door to her bedroom. The bathroom at the end of the hall. The living room is deep, dark, broken up by brown hills, brighter corners, saturated with a kind of powder: the unchanged air has formed a sediment, fills the space, filters the glow from outside. The street lamps drape the windows in orange gauze. The rug is cut in two: in the light, the knights, the huts, the profiles with long hair; in the far end of the room, the real floral patterns, the semidarkness. She holds out her hands, feeling her way toward the familiarity of things, the sofa, the mirror on the mantelpiece, the four-legged table suckled by chairs, the big, squat lamp. The cracks in the floor tiles have grown larger, breaking the seams through the middle to form eyelids, ears, smiles scattered over the ground. The dog's nose and the boar's snout are facing her, almost identical knots in the wood, on the doors of the sideboard. Her footsteps make no sound, she concentrates on breathing, on moving through the fluffy air. She recognizes the poplar at her bedroom window, and the clowns lined up by size, wide awake on her pillow. When she returns, her father is sitting in the living room, he's in pajamas but seems to have just come back from a trip. She runs to him; he appears to be asleep. His eyelids are closed but his eyes show through, bluish, translucent, without pupils, and in their depths she can still see him, his face upside down as in the back of a tiny spoon. It's the terror that wakes her up. The French door creaks, for a second she doesn't understand, and the sea tosses beneath the windows back home: the waves break where the poplar whispered, rolling in at the foot of the apartment building, licking the old

iron railings, spitting salt spray on the numbers of the
door-code panel. Then it's like a second awakening,
the feeling of being put back in place, of knowing once
more exactly where she is: here, in front of the sea, at
the interface of the world. She climbs the stairs to the
apartment of the man on the thirteenth floor. The staircase is in raw concrete, bare beneath the small orange
light. Sometimes the building shakes itself, you'd think
it was the breakers, but it's the elevator: the machines
make the weights oscillate in the shafts. The man seems
surprised. Her mother is not at his place. She accepts
an ice cream, not a good ice cream, a watery one. You
hear the waves and the elevator in alternation as if, on
the top floor, the building's two arcs came together: the
pendulum of the machines, the to-and-fro of the sea.
He asks her where her mother is. She sees the telephone
number, written in her head, learned by heart along
with the prohibition against accepting candy: you are
lost, kidnapped, you've been found all the way across
the country, somebody's hurt you, you went to the
wrong school, got on the wrong métro, you got sick far
from home. But the image immediately goes dark, like
an unplugged TV. She moves away from the screen for
a moment, steps back a few feet, then moves closer as
if by surprise, with her eyes wide open—but there's
nothing where what she learned by heart it should be,

nothing but a hole that goes on forever. She looks for lines, sounds, an echo (but there's no word on the tip of her tongue, only a hint of a rhythm, ten digits, all possible). She sees her father get up, however, knocking over an object that blocks his way, and search through the piled-up shadows for a telephone he cannot find. He stands there, pale, frightened. Darkness surrounds him, slowly reclaims him, he calls out, the dust motes whirl around, shadows erase him, consume him, and she loses him in the shifting of the furniture, in the incoherent night, as if she were peering into troubled water, through which drifts to the surface, from freshly disturbed algae, a turbid cloud shaped like a seahorse. The man has stood up; the sea is getting impatient, throwing handfuls of water at the windows; he stays out on the balcony, leaning on the railing. The rain begins to plaster down his hair. The top of his shirt darkens, his trousers stick to his buttocks, drops hang from the bottom of his jaw.

He wipes a hand across his face, grips the guardrail; the iron is wet, grainy. The weather has suddenly changed. The bistro owners bring in their tables, the windows are steamed up, the different muffled musics sputter in the storm; it's probably those lights—blurry and perhaps more festive like that, facing the wilderness of waves—that distress him so, as though he were a castaway. The range of possibilities is not large: the bars on the beach, along the main drag; unless he took her straight to his place, up on the cliff, in the surfers' neighborhood. The rain is winding down, the kid is watching him through the plate glass blistered with drops of water and light, but he'll be perfect in his assigned role: the babysitter with ice cream in the freezer.

The cormorants are asleep, gothic and black in the lighthouse beam. Tourists are leaving the Corsaire, the port is deserted, the blacktop glistens. The cormorant is a seabird with permeable feathers, obliged to dry out between dives, wings stretched like an umbrella. She hangs on Patrick's arm, laughing at random; she's never sure if he's joking or not. Through the misted-over window of the bistro they've entered she sees the tall apartment building, locates the studio thanks to the neighbor's light, above and to the right; she'll stay another five minutes. Every night the façade is brighter and brighter, as more and more apartments are occupied. When she arrived, the neighbor was like a lighthouse keeper, alone on his balcony, perched there like a bird. In less than two weeks she is supposed to leave, when the building will have illuminated all its compartments, like an Advent calendar for June. She runs her fingers through her hair, chasing the idea away.

She's conscious of Patrick's gaze, of her taut shoulder straps, the curve of her breasts beneath the fabric, her exposed armpit. She agrees to another beer, and after that she's going to leave. The bar is warm, humid, with a smell mingling tobacco and seaweed; the table at which they finally sit is covered with a film of salt and water. She's given a napkin; Patrick has ordered her an assortment of local specialties, he knows the owner, they grab each other's arms, laughing. The ham tastes like an old purse. Patrick clinks glasses with her; she smiles at him, bends her neck, her hair tumbles silkily. She feels she's confusing (and perhaps that's it, suddenly, that urgency) the desire to wedge his masculine hips between her thighs with the desire to be alone, alone with her breasts, her skin, her hands. Shiny with wear, her dress is as damp as her face, not from sweat but from steam. The door is ajar; a cool draft sometimes wafts by her knees. She should go home, but the sound of the sea and that heavy marine humidity make it seem that nothing could happen, that no one could ever be left entirely alone here. He takes her outside and into his arms on the top of the cliff. She can see the roof of the big apartment house, it seems to lord it over the entire city. His saliva is salty. Their cheeks stick together, their hair sparkles with water droplets. She loves this numbness, the lips obliterated by the crush of contact, the face that fills up, melts into the body, which turns round as the mouth descends, sinks in, embeds itself in the flesh while the limbs, multiplied and curved, flop back around a center that swells into prominence. The octopus, hunting the spiny lobster among the rocks it calls home, glues itself in a star shape over the niche; its large head can be seen swaying in the current over the patiently waiting beak. Trapped, the spiny lobster waits, until hunger makes it forgetful. It tries to leave; the beak strikes between head and thorax, at a joint in the carapace, paralyzing the victim alive within its shell, which is sucked clean, to the exasperation of spear fishermen. They walk along; she likes the space he leaves between them, the wet asphalt, the intermittent flash of the lighthouse, the great horizontal flight that sweeps the face of the city. The crowns of the tamarisks appear and disappear, tangled against the sky and then plucked back by the cliff. From time to time she draws closer and Patrick slows down; the light is so bright that both of them stagger when the beam hits them, as though a third body were hugging them. She can make out, in its glare, the texture of his skin, the pores fine-stitched by the salt and the sun. The days are so long, she's seeing the night for the first time, a night in June, so short that she's in a rush. He rings a doorbell, their bodies flicker in the beam before the door opens onto a hallway, people, music and lights, they're in a club, not his place at all. She hadn't listened to a thing he was saying. He kisses some girls, kneads some shoulders, shakes hands across the bar. Guys are laughing, leaning back, they have the same yellow hair as Patrick's, the same knotty forearms, the same loose, colorful clothing. The music pounds in your chest. Two very young girls are dancing in very short skirts; smoke rises peacefully through the lights, winding around their childish hips, lazily encircling the mirrored disco balls. Some lycée students are sitting next to her, they roll a joint, hold it out to her, shout a question; probably, Where is she from? Or else, How long has she known Patrick? She looks around for him, he waves to her, his teeth are stupidly white in the purple neon light, and the contour of his neck, below his perfect jawline, is enough to make you scream. He's bent tenderly over some guy, yelling in his ear, it must be surfer talk, English terms for various waves and the movements of their boards. She stands up; a cool mist floats around one group, that's where the door is. The sea is fresh, incisive. Her ears are ringing; each wave rolls in there and breaks, wresting her free. She goes through the tamarisks, down the cliff, on the narrow old-fashioned flights of stairs. The fake wood is so old that the iron pokes out below the molded hand rails: long, bare tendons, red and salt-corroded in their concrete bark. The building's bulk surprises her, looming up blackly, cutting off a flight of fancy on the stairs: one of those terraces where, ever so long ago, crinolines capped by parasols were allowed out in the sun. A modern platform of lightweight steel is grafted onto the amputated terrace and winds at length around the building. It's a kind of scaffolding, emergency stairs for a major disaster; she has already explored them in daylight with the child, suspended in the sky, discovering what's on the other side of the one where they live. The guano makes it a trifle slippery, sometimes you disturb a few birds. The waterfront seems narrow through the tiny openings in the metal floor; the sea rolls beneath her feet. The waves advance, line after line of them, rounded toward the opposite curve of the beach, so that from above it looks like a huge X, a hyperbola, and you wonder how the join is made, or what prodigious passages open up between the water and the world. The sky is a silvery black, glinting with clouds. A plane flies by, the last plane of the evening, the connection for transatlantic flights. The rain is advancing, as though the sky were drawing nearer, wrapping its depth into a great fold that constantly shakes loose, rippling and shuddering; the squall comes ever closer, stirred up in the bottom of a colossal cauldron, making visible what had been unseen: wind, air. Now she hears the noise, the boiling and hissing, a hundred thousand live coals heating the sea and blowing up gusts. The waves have become mute things crushed by the tide on high, you see the edge coming on, you see the foaming sky. She braces herself, gets ready. The wave passes over her, in one second she's drenched, slammed up against the wall by the shock. Access to the balconies is closed off, she has to turn back. She can make out the tamarisks, thick with shadows; she proceeds quickly, dripping, out of breath. The metallic clang of her footsteps is immediately absorbed by the squall. She's starting to feel cold. With the dense, brutal rain the night has become completely black, booming and thunderous. She runs her hand along the rail, feels the steps beneath her feet; no light at all breaks through anymore, only a strange softness (swift, periodic) arrives at moments to slow down the wind—probably the remnants of the lighthouse's glory. A streaming claw strikes her face; she has found the trees again, and the cliff. The small staircase is a cascade of muddy water. She leans against the tree trunks. She can't see a thing anymore, not behind her, not over by the apartment building, not under the trees in the din of the rain, in that forest growing—black and crackling—from the firestorm of the sea. Someone is there. Someone is waiting for her beneath the leaves. She sees him now, she can make out the bright spot of his face, the dark stroke of the shoulders, the white fists. It's him. Her heart stops. He takes her by the elbow; she feels the cold, wet fingers, she has no excuse, a husband, a father, it's all there, she has to follow him. He asks her where she's been; he was looking all over for her. She's laughing now, she abandons herself to the amnesia of those arms: let him carry her off, let him take her. It's Patrick. For the first time he asks questions. Back at his place he talks to her about Australia, Wollongong, Twofold Bay, he has friends over there, he's going. They laugh: that's a lot of water to cross. Their hair has dried, he puts down his glass, he comes over. Afterward, she will get dressed again, he will pick up his sentence where he left off; his blue eyes will sparkle like an ocean wave in an air-freshener commercial. Perhaps he'll propose Australia to her. Toward the back of the city the clouds will have whitened, though the waves will still be black; the night will withdraw, cold and westbound, to the bottom of the sea, leaving pale seaweed beached beneath the sky; she will walk, slowly, skirting with dreamy steps the immense absence of the sea.

5

There aren't many people at the beach yet. He jogs down to get as close as possible to the waves, spreads out the towel from his hotel, and goes right into the water. The swim trunks he brought with him were so old that when he put them on, the elastic gave way, crumbling like parchment; he had to buy a new pair at the local Galeries Lafayette. The water is freezing; he feels like screeching, he hops around, each little jump slashing his ankles. Big breakers collapse a yard away, piling onto the horizon, dragging it down across the sand, pulling long streaks of bright sky after them, regaining strength, always rising again. He advances cautiously, watching for that very brief moment of the wave when it catches the sun: just beneath the crest, before it rolls over. A turquoise transparency, precious, fleeting, immediately swept away. He's in up to his knees, the current pulls one way, then the other; the sea in that spot is white with darting green blotches. A few swimmers slip between two waves and resurface with ease farther out, beyond the boiling surf, laughing crazily. In one swoop the universe turns topsy-turvy, the beach pounces on him, the sky coils up, a skin splits, shed like a glove turned inside out: space has caved in at the center, releasing a cannibal sap—he's being tasted, something is trying to ingest him, but finally the breakers vomit him up. The sand of the depths has left a long red mark on his belly; it's a little too rough around here. He laughs all alone, hiccuping; a colony of sea urchins has moved into his sinuses, he coughs and spits, and spies a kind of gigantic puddle where he can discreetly jettison the sand now weighing down his trunks.

The sun has come to rest here, on this smooth surface; the water is deep, calm, and warm. He wiggles his toes, so white in the limpid water, detached from his feet, zigzagging next to his calves, his thighs jutting from his stomach, plexus overhanging various scattered pieces. He closes his eyes. Basks. The round mass of water sways, gently pressing his body; he floats unaided, leaning on the water, in its delicate motion; he is part of the beach, the sea, and everything swaying in the sea. As he drifts off to sleep, in the hum of waves farther along jostling bathers who squawk like seagulls, something stops him at the edge of slumber; something like a memory, a tiny anxiety. In the dream just getting under way, still moored to the morning by the blue of the sea, the yellow of the beach, the fancy red hotel, he sees the lighthouse, pointing distinctly, a

cylinder so bright it throbs and vibrates in broad daylight: three, four, five lighthouses against the thunder-
struck sky. The bathers' cries draw a new shrillness
from the waves, a harsh, eddying note; he breathes
underwater, astonished but unafraid, watching the
waves curl upside down, in the brief green light: the
ceiling rises, explodes outward, overflowing, drawn by
a sudden force pulling on the top of the world. The
whistling persists, grows louder, brings him back to
shore. He opens his eyes; a guy in red swim trunks is
gesturing at the edge of the water. Lifeguard, it's written all over his chest. He rights himself clumsily. The
air feels icy. The guy is talking to him about still waters, fishy currents, especially one called the *baïne* that
captures, drowns, destroys, sluicing out pockets of water as if pulling a drain plug. Meekly, he complies. He
has always hated cops.

They are to meet at flood tide for her first waves. She's
early, bending over the shallow pools among the rocks.
Her mother has been renting a cabana and a deck chair
for the past few days; she bought a pretty bathing suit,
a scarf she ties around her hair, and some large dark
glasses; she smokes, she smiles at her; she's so pretty
that looking at her too much almost makes your heart
ache. The rock pools are sheets of glass, windows on

the world below: you see how crabs sidle across tiny deserts; how translucent shrimp, perched on canyons, frolic with wild leaps that contract their intestines, straight lines onto which are slipped seven rings of aqueous flesh; how periwinkles roll to the foot of silt screes and, all in a dither, readjust their opercula; how astonishing, frightening, and easy it is to dare dip in a finger and for no good reason at all provoke disasters in this universe. Her mother is still there, in the deck chair; she has tipped back her head. Behind her dark glasses her eyes are doubtless closed; her face is un-clouded, blind, welcoming the sun, like an open hand, a face from which all shadows have unreservedly fled to crowd into the hollow between her breasts. On the sleek body, set off by the bathing suit, there is no longer anything but this black triangle, this eye-catching me-dallion that makes her visible, recognizable, and dis-turbing beyond all other women. A few sea urchins with air bubbles pearling among their spines keep watch underwater: stern, suspicious, inaccessible. The anemones are viscous, shutting savagely at a touch: merely grazing their long fluorescent lashes makes them retract behind their red eyelids, after which you must wait, as patiently as possible, for something in there to decide, or to forget, and for these big empty eyes to open wide again under the sea. She checks, her mother is still there in the canvas chair; simply by running a few steps she could be immediately beside her: vacant, fathomless, laid out flat on her back by the sun. She sprinkles water over the fine crust of shells on a dried-out rock, and they open like magic squares, spitting and effervescing, confident of the rising tide. She glances around; no one, including her mother, is watching her. She tramples the anemones, it's harder than she'd thought, her shoe sole slips off them, rubber on rubber. There's nothing inside, just this flayed muscle, no eyelashes, no light, not even squished guts. Big empty shells have bleached around the puddle like bones; they look like souvenirs, heavy in the hand, like stones; grandmother had some at home, you could hear the sea inside. She sticks a finger in the water, dispelling her reflection; then the circles close up again, a very fine dust settles to the bottom, and her face comes back together: her eyes, nose, mouth, reunited on the jelly of the water. She returns slowly across the sand; her mother has sat up in the chair and is talking to Patrick.

She was awakened by the arrival of breakfast, brought by a chambermaid, or a nurse, in a blue-striped smock. She used to rise with the sun, and now she is as if possessed by sleep. On the bedside table, she has placed a framed photo of the child, the same one she had on the television. She sips a little coffee, nibbles on a croissant. Something in her body is crushing her, restraining her; she's like a heavy beast that's been sleeping, curled around itself, for several days. In the summer, when there's no school, and the child has been dropped off early in the morning by her mother before work, they take a train to the forest. They order lemonades at the refreshment stands; strollers and children's scooters arrive from the chic suburbs bordering on the woodland; climbers in rubber slippers silently overtake them, heading for rock faces to which they will cling with their long spider-monkey arms. Farther along, on a slab of limestone, the two of them eat cubes of cheese and apples cut into quarters. The sun spreads out in the vapor exhaled by the foliage; the world is enveloped in a fleecy pillowcase of pale yellow that muddles the black tree trunks, erases branches, rubs out paths; they bathe in these wisps, in this woolly air where the sunbeams melt together, swelling from the pressure of the day. The wind, slowly, makes its way. The capped earth pillars, the White Lady, the tall rock chimneys glide above the trees. The shouts of children reach them from very far away, through that thick milt of light. The forest is silent; the birds prefer the clearings. The two of them admire, on the flat faces of stones, the presence of fossils: spirals, little chiseled chambers, the valvules of vanished shells. The sea receded, the mud caught them in its matrix, and their flesh was consumed, abandoning, as humus for the primeval undergrowth, only the impression of their passage. She explains to the child that it's here that the city was built, in the quarries, its walls the archives of the sea, sliced up by the stonecutters. In the streets, on the way home, they keep an eye out for the coiled shells of ammonites, and the lines drawn beneath the porches, with dates, to mark the floods. From the woods to the city, the afternoon accompanies them with a seamless light along the deserted streets, a light as warm and raspy as a voice. The child, in the photo, has that tanned look of summer. She had just come back from the mountains, she'd never seen the sea. He used to say it was healthier, quieter, less touristy in the mountains. She tried to show her the sea, in the woods, from the top of the White Lady, where nothing protects the branches from the sun, where everything—the foliage, all the varieties of trees, even the clearings—blends together and flattens out in the glare. Then the sea appears, so vast that the curvature of the Earth becomes visible. The child smiles, holding her hand. Television gave her the general idea, while the forest shows her the movement, and the wind, space, froth, and pollen suggest the swell. She breathes, drinks, enjoys herself gazing at the phantom sea.

That photo—she was the one who took it. The child

has a faraway look, seems slightly disoriented; back in the city, parents off at work; she talks only grudgingly about the trip, not saying exactly what she wants. The two of them had returned to their routine. There were ten days left before the beginning of school, time enough to make sure she still knew how to read and write, time to go back to the forest. Iridium is a white metal from outer space; its presence on Earth is due only to the chance plummetings of stars. There is one stratum, sometimes found weathering out, that contains these nuggets with the rainbow name. Above this iridized stratum, there are no fossils of dinosaurs, which is the main argument for the thesis that they vanished because of a meteorite. In the afternoon, tired from their walks, falling asleep on the sofa, she and the child watched them collapse on television under a black sun, as ash from the meteorite, mingling with dust from the impact, slowly buried their agony. They went to visit them, in the museum, on rainy days. The child trotted, tiny and well-informed, among the big bodies frozen in midstride, among their claws, teeth, feet, among those impossible cold-blooded machines with eye sockets larger than the human skull, and yet she was merry, self-assured, walking jauntily by stone skeletons in dioramas, where the duck-headed iguanodon wades around on two hind legs in what will become a forest. The child knew all about absences, they didn't faze her, but she would stop, dumbfounded, before the jars of fetuses. As for her, she would discover old memories, an ancient trust in things; she saw herself again, accepting these marvels, and she was proud of bequeathing them, of participating, persevering after death, still giving life to the child, since through this boundless legacy she never ceased belonging to her. From her bed, she gazes out across the balcony at the spectacle of the denuded ground, torn open through its geological periods: the petrified sapwood of the cliff, where the Earth, like an old tree, inscribes time circle by circle. The hotel TV station explains the benefits of thalassotherapy: long, lithe bodies luxuriate in various saline muds and then stretch out, coated and cosseted, in impeccable white dressing gowns. The masseuse is waiting to wrap her in seaweed. It seems to her that she will be staying there a very long time, floating in sargasso, unable to leave the room and the cliff.

"Here we go": that's all he can think. He looks this way and that at the photo in his hand; he doesn't really get it: how can he ask this guy—with wet hair, in baggy bathing trunks with Day-Glo stripes, who pulled the photo out of a Galeries Lafayette bag bulging with a sandy towel—if he's from the police? Has he questioned other agencies, the hotels? When he tries to give back the photo, the guy grabs his arm. It can't be her husband. A husband would seem less calm and be better dressed. Take another look, says the guy. She's in semi-profile, summery, draped in her hair; it's a picture that doesn't tell him anything, a picture of the light around her, the space she occupies, the lines of her face. It's hard to make out her surroundings, blurred by the wind and her hair; leaves, perhaps. Where is it? What has she done? What justifies this type of inquiry? He'd like to see a photo of her house, her husband, her dog, her parents; a photo of her in winter, in autumn; one of her childhood, her school. He'd like to see a photo of her when she's old, and after she goes away. He'd like to see her making love. He'd like to see her crying, raging, suffering. He'd like to see her change over time. If this guy here, sitting in front of him, were an agent for a somewhat special insurance company, he'd sign up immediately with a contract guaranteeing him, for life, news of her, pictures of her, through clairvoyance or omnipresence. Frightened, finally showing some emotion, she hastily gathers up her belongings: that bathing suit she just bought, her scarf, the child's few things—without a word for him, of course, without a thank-you, but running to the door he shows her (and opens for her), following him down the fire escape on the side of the building; the walls vibrate, the guy's about to leave the elevator, he warned them in the nick of time. Then, the car, he will have rented a car. They'll go south, they'll take the ferry at the tip of the continent. The guy is standing up, he takes back the photo, leaves his cell-phone number. In three days, at most, he'll have figured out that the only hangout in the city, its center, its main event, is the beach: he'll see her, he'll recognize her, plunked there, idiotically, while the kid plays a few yards away with their pet surfer. He will compare her features with the face in the photo and find them the same. He's outside now, pretending to read the notices in the window, unless he's enjoying the sun, hands in the pockets of his baggy swim trunks. He wonders if he should call the guy back, talk with him some more. He'd like simply to give her the message, have her know what he's done for her, keeping quiet about her, just like that, for nothing. After all, she still hasn't paid up for June, and he could kick her out now, it's almost July.

With the ten thousand francs from the savings account plus, let's say, fifteen thousand from the sale of the car, ten thousand if she made a bad deal, from which you subtract two months' rent for the security deposit, and assuming she's paying three thousand francs a month—she can hold out all summer, unless she's switched to the weekly rate, which begins, according to a small poster below the display window, on

July 1. He can picture her rather easily in the décor of the model apartment, having tea between the yellow curtains, in front of the blue sea; or in the garden of that house, calling the dog, getting ready to rejoin a smiling husband carrying a child on his shoulders. Two million for a house; he's not going to be moving here any time soon. The synthetic fabric of his trunks is already dry, and he can feel the sun through his T-shirt. He'll treat himself to an ice cream. The guy in the real estate agency is pretending to read a file, he knows that woman so well he couldn't think of anything else during the entire interview, like the way alcoholics, in the middle of a conversation, can't help following the bartender with their eyes. The ice cream vendor knows her too, definitely. He shakes his plastic bag, blows sand off the photo. He could spend some time here, with his wife's photo. A widower, alone—people would whisper a few discreet words behind his back. He'd have the right to stay there by the sea. It's 81 degrees. The sun is taking up all the space. The ice cream man is talking about the lovely weather and the ideal temperature for business. His name is Lopez. He's a half man, in a little booth. He watches the tide come in, go out. He must know the extreme range of the equinoxes, the level the water can reach by stretching or contracting, like a big muscle. He must know on which day, and at which hour, such-and-such a rock emerges or disappears, he must have noticed tendencies, inclinations, long periods of time when the sea is grayer, greener, rough or swollen, dull or sparkling, beneath a sky that lets more or less daylight slip through. Or else the sea is only a background, the verso of the city, a given as elementary as a clement temperature for selling ice cream, a bit of blue glimpsed between people's heads on sunny, crowded days, while Lopez waits for the winter months to regain the use of his legs.

He is sitting on a bench, enjoying his ice cream. Lopez is leaning forward unobtrusively, watching him. He's in no hurry. The waterfront is well patrolled. He'll be able to ask all the questions he wants, of Lopez, the lighthouse keeper, the lifeguards, the tearoom waiters, the fishermen, the man who rents out cabanas and beach chairs. Few places in the world are scanned by so many eyes. It's almost a surprise, a slight disappointment, not to find anyone familiar in the photo, any sign of complicity with this place, something he could pinpoint clearly. The locks of hair are immobilized in the light; she's a woman who doesn't know a thing, who isn't planning to go anywhere, who'd never imagine a breakup, absence, kidnapping. The wisps of hair hover motionless around her. She's risking prison for child abduction—not to mention the loss of her civil rights—if she continues her flight, but you won't see it in her face. He'll run into her, she'll glide by him, in that sunny seaside obliviousness, in the light in the photo-graph. He looks up; people are strolling, roller-blading, walking dogs, chatting. He had thought, for a moment, that he was alone. But he knows them all. They could all recognize her, all confirm the absolute identity of that face.

Yesterday, trying on bathing suits in the Galeries Lafayette, she was startled by the marks of the sun she saw in the mirror: two slender white lines crossed on her back, pale legs, very brown arms; her hair is blonder; her palms, hollows in the matte surface of her hands, are as rosy as the lip of a seashell, while the heels of her tanned feet are orange, polished by the sand. She doesn't understand how she could have got-ten darker so quickly. Being careful with the sanitary strip in the crotch of the new bathing suits has re-minded her that she has her period, that she'd made an appointment, she seems to recall, for sometime in June, a routine checkup. She leans back against the mirror, which feels cold; it's pleasant in the store. The child is playing ghost in the dressing-room curtains. Standing with her legs planted wide apart, she sees that her thighs are thinner, veined with pink and blue, soft—especially near her sex—from being concealed so long beneath the dress, while the tanned skin of her arms, shoulders, and back is rougher. She stays leaning against the rear wall of the cubicle awhile, crumpling a bathing suit in her hands, calm, astonished to be so alone, so feather-light, immortal. Now, as she lies in the beach chair, areas left pale by the dress can be seen beneath the straps of the new suit, especially just above her breasts, where she's turning pink, but the dividing line will soon be gone. The sun goes through the skin, deliciously warming and dilating the lungs and other organs; she vaguely recalls—she's heard it said—that tubercular patients used to sunbathe like this, in reclining chairs, on balconies at the seashore, even in winter, muffled up in elegant plaid blankets, chatting half-heartedly, immensely fatigued, and with a book that was always too heavy threatening to fall from their hands. It seems the winter here is rainy, and that, people say, is why the countryside inland is so green. Consumptives preferred the Mediterranean, oleanders, the scent of almonds and orange blossoms. She roots around for the sunblock lotion in the Galeries Lafayette bag. There's some fruit for the child, a sweater in case she gets chilly after her swim, a large towel from the apartment, and the English grammar she borrowed from Patrick's place, along with a Walkman that he obviously didn't use. With a halfway decent memory, it doesn't take long to get your English back.

*   *   *

They've come to get her on her balcony for her seaweed massage. She was watching the mirages out at
sea, the islands born of the sunshine's vibrations,
rather like bouquets, balancing on a single stem, that
blossom into broad shadows hovering above the horizon. Just as it's difficult, in foggy weather, to know
whether the mountain range extends far out to sea or
whether it's a cloud, solidly sculpted, mimicking a lofty
peak, likewise she no longer knows if the islands exist,
blurred by the light, or if the ocean is wide open here,
facing America, a due West throwing its mirages up
over the Earth's rim. Perhaps the planet has veered off
its axis, bowing its blue head toward the sun; the
magma has shifted, throwing gravity off center and
skewing the rotations of the Earth, which wobbles like
a freighter listing and wallowing from its cargo. They
hoist her out of her reclining chair. She resists; there's a
group of children on the beach, she'd like to get a good
look at them; they tell her it's the season for class trips,
that she must snap out of her lethargy, move around,
participate, they won't be bringing her meals up to her
room anymore. She falls asleep in the bath; the seaweed unravels in the heated salt water, cooking, thick-
ening; she no longer feels her legs under the long slimy
ribbons, her hands are corals, her arms dead eels, and

her breasts moonfish that float, slackly, beneath the
drifting net of her skin. The mermaid is a mythological
animal familiar to all cultures: half woman, half fish,
or sometimes half bird; skin, hair, scales, or feathers;
enchantress or victim, sliced in half, quartered, cleft by
desire. Christopher Columbus's sailors confused her
with the manatees of the grassy deltas of the Indies; the
females have breasts and broad, welded thighs. The
human race seeks a balance between walking upright
(hands free, narrow pelvis) and childbearing (wide pelvis); quadrupeds give birth quickly, without suffering,
and the Sirenia are born on the bosom of the waves. If
she had it all to do over, she'd eagerly make the same
mistake and ask again for legs. Her thoughts are in a
whirl, maybe she's getting senile. And yet, she's been
doing mnemonic exercises for a long time now: she
learns verses, lists, revisits the museums of her youth
room by room. In her son-in-law's presence, she was
able to reconstruct that entire last afternoon spent with
the child, up to her daughter's arrival, the blue dress
with the crossed straps, and that position, the body
standing limply at the sink, the thin stream of water;
she could remember the precise angle of the sunlight
striking the tiled floor, and the back of that neck,
through which no command, no impulse seemed to
move. But she hasn't come up with a single useful detail, a word she might have said, a wish, a curse, some-

thing a little peculiar, or anything at all for the investigation; she didn't know what to tell her son-in-law, how to describe the vacancy of the body, and that light, so intense it seemed to flicker; what was needed was a photo, a photo of her memory, a beam shining through her skull and projecting her recollections on a screen. Her legs seem to have melted beneath their weight, her body has leaked away; she tries to open her eyes and there's nothing anymore but that gelatinous, lukewarm sensation, what amnesiacs must find instead of memory itself. Still, she'd be able to remember everything, the living and the dead, bring back forms striding along, set houses upright, recall words, until that specific episode, that parenthesis, that gap; she'd need only to stop, choose a time frame, select a case, grasp the essentials and understand, but everything streams past, flowing along, and suffering bobs about like a cork. They're lifting her up again, she feels a pain beneath her ribs, the light is green, rippling, as in an aquarium, the Museum of the Sea is, along with the cliff, the jewel of the city, turtles, octopuses, seahorses, dolphins, seals from the ocean that were sick or caught in nets, sharks in fine fettle flown in from Florida. She's cold, she must be out of the seaweed. She'd like to pull herself together again, put back her arms, legs, she sees a hand, her smooth and slender hand, her smooth and slender legs, her light, round breasts, that remembered body that could also wear elegantly, on the same young shoulders, blue dresses with crossed straps. That's how the child will grow up: tall, thin, as though fathers had no effect on this lineage of square hips, small breasts. She'd like to move but bits of her life are stirring, sluggishly, tingling faintly: childhood in the palm of her hand, adolescence in the bend of her arm, adulthood in the faint, far-off jolts in her chest. Memories are dismembering her, it's this disease that's attacking her— the one that, far from drying up her memory and its images, is making a tumor of time where her body ought to be.

6

He calls the client. He tells him, basically, the truth: that he's on the right track, that she's here. He doesn't go into detail, talks about the climate, the effects of the border, mentions witnesses; he asks for a little more time, and in particular for those precise instructions one discusses only at the end: What does he want, exactly? The client says he wants the child, just the child. That he won't press charges. That he wishes to be left in peace. He takes a shower; smokes, wrapped in his towel, out on the hotel balcony. Something is giving way in the sky; the sun is slowly slipping. He gets dressed; the room is still bright, just a hint of shadow in the corners, and through the open window the day throws a square of colors on the wall. The window frame quivers. The breeze swoops down on the afternoon, with reds, browns, ochers; the sea stretches out. He shaves, sprinkles on some lavender water. The open sea surges into the room through the three panels of the mirror. He behaves like someone getting ready to go out. He's forming habits. He has no appointments. He's going to have a drink on the casino terrace. The room grows even larger as the sun draws closer, its rays entering head-on, opening out walls and ceiling; the sea encroaches on the city and the sky. He hears children shouting on the beach, a class trip, recent arrivals, they're splashing around within a floating line of buoys; gathered up when the ropes are pulled in, they shriek with vexation in their net. In the distance, over the steady rhythm of the waves, between the blue mirror and the open window throwing its glare on the wallpaper, the cries whirl like a flight of slow birds. The walls drift lightly; the wind is warm, supple, and the curtains flutter. The lighthouse has come on, its lamp is barely brighter than the sky, the beam gliding over the untouched shadows. When he closes the door of his room, the lighthouse follows him through the halls. The sky has taken on a mauve hue, and a threadbare Moon, quite pale, seems to be at the bottom of a stained-glass window. He could go down every evening like this, freshly dressed, along the cliff, to see how the tamarisks are doing, check on the guardrail, say hello to Lopez, take a seat on the waterfront terraces: the one at the pâtisserie, the one at the casino, the one where the orchestra plays during the tourist season. He'd join the Cormorant Club, and all year long, in every kind of weather, he would take a dip in the ocean. Ordering his beer in front of the violet sea squeezed and rumpled by the evening, he wonders what makes a memory. This moment, in the rush of others, when he touches his lips to the froth, when the sea gives the silken rustle he thinks of as the sound of endless change, when the wind gently stirs hair and lifts up skirts—will he remember it? Will he remember this very same sky, this sun, this horizon? This lighthouse and this Moon, stubbornly present at the rendezvous? These craters, whose outlines can be seen, and the Sea of Tranquility, the Sea of Fertility, where the striped boot prints of the astronauts must still be visible? When he lets go, he sees, as if by surprise, people, and especially places—such and such a precise instant in this or that garden—without having had any indication at the time that that moment would become a memory, and without successive interpretations changing the image it leaves behind, gradually clearing away superimposed accents, inflexions, expressions, climates. He wonders what he will see when he remembers the ocean; and whether one can remember it as one does a garden or a face, keeping a single motionless, fixed moment of it, a moment never seen, never experienced, but that isn't an abstract of the rest; a moment of real time, empty but familiar, that gels as if in a mold, contracting into an object, a vignette, a fetish. She has just sat down, at a table next to his, he recognizes her, he doesn't even need to turn his head. She's alone. The child must be playing over by the water, she looks up from her reading now and then. Her gaze stops between book and sea, her lips part slightly, she looks as if she were praying. She's wearing little earphones on her head. From time to time her fingers move in the folds of her dress, pushing buttons. Her hair is red in the sunset, her cheeks still full of daylight. Her identity is so clear that a lump comes to his throat. He stands up, lets himself be carried away by the vast nonsense of the sea, by those waves, by that summery music. Smiling, he pulls out the chair in front of her.

For one second, she's convinced she knows him, her heart races, her cheeks burn, she interrupts her English lesson. But he merely asks if he can sit down, that's all, buy her a drink, she hardly hears him through the foam earpieces, she pushes Play again. He doesn't insist, goes back to his own table, almost as if he were waiting; or he's doing like everyone else, he's looking at the sea, the women, taking advantage of his vacation. The child will be back soon. She pays for her coffee, gets up, walks to the edge of the water. Her heart gradually stops pounding.

She's never been so close before, it's quaking, shuddering beneath her feet. The water pulls away, spreads out, seems to increase: between the mass that has just collapsed, the froth that boils and seethes, there, close enough to touch her, and the surface rising behind it, sucking in and scooping out—it stretches, looking like the inside of a mollusk, steely blue, veined with white, an oyster, the underside of a tongue; it yawns without breaking, it's smooth, glossy, the lining of an organ they must pass through. They move closer still, Patrick's hand is crushing hers, they've planted their feet in the foam and already the curl is sucking them in, they have to stand with their legs wide apart, bracing themselves. She looks at the other swimmers, the ones who hesitate rigidly on the edge, and those who are already on the other side; no one stays in the curl, no one can survive in the curl, in that void the waves exhaust themselves trying to fill, where the water somersaults, swells, then disappears, where air cracks, sand explodes, where nothing subsides or fills up. Patrick has dashed in still holding on to her; her arm is dislocated, her body crashes into the water (lemmings are small arctic rodents that leap en masse from the tops of ice banks), he told her not to breathe, to hold her breath tightly, even babies do that naturally (but they've kept opercula like sea lions have), all around her it's white, snowy, she's the tiny figure shaken up in a snow globe (don't breathe, let the heart beat), one day she'll try oxygen tanks and her lungs, by themselves, will join together water and earth. Suddenly everything grows brighter. The water is a big green eye glued to her eye, she sees into the depths of the watery pupil, through to the water's brain, the bubbles, the convolutions, the vortices, the uncertainties; then something tugs at her as if the sea wanted to call her back, resolve an ambiguity, a question, a doubt; Patrick holds on to her, she's clamped belly-down to the seabed, she's a flatfish and what she glimpses of her skin is sand-colored, then everything lifts off (what astronauts feel in their shuttle is no more violent), the sea swirls above her, rips the water, something falls away far behind, she is the extreme tip of this batting eyelash, and the hard, crushed, compact sand slides away beneath her: the eye opens.

The sky is enormous, much larger than the sea. The sky doesn't touch her, keeps its distance, and the shore seems already so remote that she realizes you drown from so much solitude, since a mere glance at the land, over there, at the houses, the terraces and the ice cream vendor, is enough to make you feel abandoned (astronauts are trained not to go insane when they see the Earth, round and blue, smaller than their porthole). Her feet are dangling beneath her body; the water is green, opaque. Around them a few severed heads are grimacing in the sun and the salt sea, catching their breath. Now past the breakers, they are high up, well beyond the cavity, safe on the shoulder of the surf. Other waves arrive, rounded waves, tall and true: ocean waves, the front of the swell. A depression curves between them, already dragging the body down, but you don't risk vanishing into the abyss anymore, just drowning. Go under! yells Patrick. Only rollers that have already broken can be crossed over the top, the body breasting the foam straight on. Otherwise you must dive, find the weak spot of the wave and break free of its suction. One moment you're escaping the sea, rediscovering the laws of the land, the body, the muscles; for one second you think you're in control—then you're beneath the whirlpool. And until you recognize the equilibrium of the sky, the light-house, the colorful row of cabanas, you fear for one dizzying instant you've found the way to the bottom of the sea.

They've passed beyond all the waves. Out where they are (resting on the ocean as on the brow of an elephant), the sea is now only an immense rocking; a long way off, heavy feet strike the ocean bottom; muscles ripple beneath the surface, shoulders roll above slopes of flat hide. The beach is dwarfed, stubby and gleaming at the bottom of the sky; from here, it seems like a migration after some cataclysm: the people are naked and tiny, massed at the edge of the water, advancing, hesitating, rushing forward; the city is de-serted. Distance is constantly shifting, she doesn't know where to look on the curve of the water. A few waves arrive on the slant from the open sea, she cranes her neck, tries to take advantage of the elephant's rolling gait. The waves break in profile, you can see the arch where surfers with salamander skin take shape in black flashes, the tube of emptiness the waves roll along and carry away. But it's difficult to truly see the wave. Should you isolate one spot in the tumbling water, mark it, following a drop, a whiteness, a brighter streak (too swift for the eye, yet slow enough for its fall to be recorded)—and return to the top again, quickly, picking out another spot, over and over, wave after wave? Or try to grasp the wave as a whole, the spume that crumbles, breaks up, scuds away in scattered threads, endlessly spreading its net over a tremendous catch: shifting, fluid, and long gone.

The ocean has become the sea, with eddies, a current that forms a swell near the coast. Warning signs become more and more violent, flesh thrashes in alarm, water spurts more quickly beneath the broad gills. The body rises and falls, the land makes its noise, breaks the water, growls, roars, lying in wait like a huge predator. Now, even if its caudal fin were curved as much as possible, open water has become inaccessible. The alarm falls silent, all is quiet in the massive movement of the waves. Fatigue has replaced hunger. The hollow beneath its worn baleen seems gradually to have closed; the sea no longer flows through it, meeting an obstacle now, a stillness, deep in the belly. The muscles needn't move to escape that hunger anymore, and the body lets itself be borne along like a buoy. In the deep, in the abyss, wait giant squid, great white corpses flushed, in sudden tremors, with lurid color. Far above, a few blue glints snag on the scales of transparent fish. Then the seaweed becomes increasingly green. Fierce, yet soothing, a breeze sweeps the water away, a cliff looms up, the light spreads out, vegetal, while blue headlands grow larger and stretch long glittering fingers toward the water. The plankton thickens, there's good grazing here, jaws wide open, swimming in the warmth and nourishment, in the tiny shrimp that suddenly seem more numerous than water droplets. The cliff marks a rock ledge; the sea is a porridge, cooking on the continental shelf. The lateral lines quiver slightly, sensing, off toward a sandy depression, the faint presence of humans, the heat of those naked seals. There are several of them, a small group in the warm water, playing with the waves near the shore. Motors cough, the water transmits brief surges; a colony has taken up residence here. Taking one last reading with its laterals, the creature avoids the beach. The cliff is quite close now, reflecting its sound waves straight back: a clayey mass, primordial, weathered by water, scarred by grottoes, runoff, faults, magnetic conglomerations, and metal fallen from the sky. Its back breaks the surface, the air is brutally dry, the wind bends its dorsal fin and drives the body toward the rollers. From now on its sonar can no longer distinguish between up and down, north and south. A boulder slices deeply into its skin. Its flanks strike the sand amid retreating waves; it suffocates slowly beneath the weight of its muscles while its gills collapse from their own volume. The land is harsh, imperious, sunken beneath its belly; the ground slues about under a motionless sun.

She twists her head around as four nurses hold her down. She's been given an injection, tended to, tucked in, seen by a specialist. There's something below the cliff, in the triangular tag-end of the tidal wash, a strange boat at the water's edge, a sailboat, perhaps. Its canvas appears to be black, as if the aged Aegeus were going to throw himself once again from the top of a cliff, and this time send the Atlantic into mourning. Because of the windows—properly closed—and the reflections on the sea, it's hard for her eyes to establish the perspective. The sail hangs, thick, dark, and limp. She'd simply like to take one last look, admire the view, study this coast, enjoy the landscape a little longer. But they say that will only wear her out even more. The tourist season is beginning, she's probably a poor advertisement for the spa. They've telephoned her son-in-law; an ambulance is coming to get her.

The basking shark is a fish of the family Squalidae that can grow to the size of a small sperm whale. It is characterized by very large gills, a collar of red grooves so deep the head seems ready to separate from the body. A harmless living fossil, toothless, filtering krill in the manner of the baleen whales, it can attain a great age, which is attested to by the concentric circles inscribed in its flesh (this can be prepared in slices, like tuna *à la basquaise,* but is little prized). It travels around the globe, solitary and openmouthed, and a recent study by the Museum of the Sea has proven that it voyages not at the mercy of the currents, as its apparent passivity and weak neuronal development might suggest, but according to strategic routes. Almost blind, like most sharks, and endowed with sensory equipment that is in fact quite sophisticated, it has a misleadingly monstrous and languid appearance that has given rise to numerous legends (mermaids, sea serpents, gigantic submarines).

It's hard to know what she's looking at, what spot

out at sea or in the empty air. Apparently she couldn't care less about that thing busy dying at the feet of all those gawkers. The local press is taking pictures; her kid has joined the schoolchildren on vacation. He's been following her since yesterday and isn't nervous at all about leaving her; he finds her again, the city or the beach always returns her. She seems to follow the same routine every day: the big apartment building, the pâtisserie, the deck chair on the beach, the casino terrace. In order to listen to the Museum of the Sea employee the reporters, the teacher, and the schoolchildren have interrupted the bucket brigade they'd formed around the shark. Big brown patches like parchment are slowly spreading, it's evaporating, soon it will dry into dust like the jellyfish that leave behind, at low tide, only a crown of black salts around a sandy well. In the meantime, the sound it's making is so distressing that he doesn't really see himself going into action with such a soundtrack, he would have preferred the waves alone, a bit of a breeze, the faraway rhythms of seaside music. The dreadful thing gasps and whimpers, you'd think it had lungs, its mouth clogged with baleen is open as wide as possible on a black and swollen tongue, trying to suck in air. A moan is heard, something childlike, human, dogs sometimes have inflections like that, it's difficult to believe that such a sound is coming from a creature so fantastically different from ourselves: it isn't an appeal, it isn't a rattle, it's a sob, the creature is sobbing. Luckily more and more seagulls are arriving, wheeling overhead by the hundreds, a brassy tempest of foam in the bend of the cliff; the employee from the Museum of the Sea must strain to be heard. She shrank back when she saw the cameras arrive. He goes over. Had he still been looking for her, having trouble finding her, the city would have produced her for him there, it's a family photograph, everyone is gathered around the sideshow attraction: the little girl obviously—he's going to have to make up his mind—as well as the tourists, the reporters, the schoolchildren, the teacher, the educational staff from the museum, a lighthouse keeper, a swimming pool attendant, bellboys from the Grand Hotel, nurses and chambermaids from the thalassotherapy center, gardeners, bistro owners, the waterfront orchestra (who have just awakened) together with some hostesses and a croupier from the casino, plus some jeering fishermen, people off pleasure boats, the lifeguards, and that movie-star surfer who takes care of the kid, and that idiot of a real estate agent who's hoping for a chance to see the mother, and the police, who are on the alert and have set up barriers to keep rubberneckers away from the crumbling cliff, and the vets from the museum (who will salvage the body with a winch, giving it the coup de grâce if need be, they're planning to stuff it), and even Lopez, who has moved his van to the top of the cliff, by the only walkway that leads to the stairs. He's right next to her now. Her ability not to see him is so great, so stubborn, that it seems to arise from a decision: after the previous day's episode she has completely ignored his presence, wearing her earphones as she drinks her coffee, lying in her deck chair with her eyes closed behind dark glasses, gazing elsewhere out on the beach. Without looking her way, he speaks to her; she says nothing. The surfer has noticed his stratagem, he's careful not to get involved. The kid has come closer, pretending to be still interested in the big fish, still part of the group of schoolchildren on vacation. He gets out his cell phone, and now the kid is fascinated.

Here they are, all three of them, coming back up. He wonders if it's the father, makes a show of stacking some cones. The little girl is frighteningly pale, he fixes her a double, chocolate-strawberry, he insists, on the house. It's the guy who thanks him, hands the ice cream to the child. Something inside her is letting go, relaxing, he knows the ice cream hasn't a thing to do with it, but still, he feels good. During the month she's been here, he's watched her turn brown, maybe grow a bit—at that age they shoot up quickly—and even learn to swim, but in a kind of astonishment, a trance from which she's beginning to emerge; perhaps she's going to cry, or laugh. If that really is the father, then he went away and came back, his wife was waiting for him, they'd agreed to meet again on the coast. Except that at least one of the suitors has been a lucky man, the whole town knows it, and this particular Penelope wasn't waiting for a man or anyone's return.

She has accepted a cone as well, and that's a first. He's curious to see which flavor she'll pick, she chooses a sorbet of course, melon, she's the type who eats just a little leaf of lettuce. The guy declines the offer with a serious, almost professional air. He's working for somebody, that guy. Maybe it's some business with spies, or blackmail, a criminal settling of scores. The coast, its reputation, its casinos, the border, they attract all sorts of people. The little girl is perhaps only an alibi, a blind, a straw child. She's a sight, the mother, sucking away at her melon ice. Her face is the same today as it was a month ago. It makes you wonder if she noticed the days going by, the weather warming, the tides rising, summer arriving, the child growing up. In one month the sky has become deep blue, the leaves on the plane trees have turned their full green, the wind has widened its embrace. The mountains have receded, blurred by the heat, palest mauve over Spain. And the sea has built up to its summer strength, derived not from storms but from constancy, the persistence of a broad and steady swell, voracious, thrusting mountains and horizon aside. The sea had to excavate as well, scouring the depths and the rock shelf, pounding all-out on the coast, which creaks in the summer with a hot, metallic grinding. It's the moment, the longest day of the year, when regrets are tossed into bonfires, when dancers leap over the glowing embers and then gather up already, in remembrance, a few cinders gone cold. The air is puffy, mild, powdery. She has that kind of skin, almost misty, as though it were loosely woven; it's as if only her dress were holding her here, in the net of its crossed shoulder straps, putting a barrier between the light and her body, which otherwise would vaporize, translucent and ethereal, in a sky full of pollen and spindrift. The sun is high in the heavens, where it waits, white and unwavering. It immobilizes the leaves of trees, the ruffled edges of waves, so curtailing gestures, so hemming in shadows, that you'd think the city was spellbound, and that this man, this woman, this child were transfixed in a solar stupor, waiting to revive, or else completely oblivious. A limousine, curtains drawn, is leaving the thalassotherapy center; the limo floats, violently white, throwing light back upon the funeral pyre of a city, beneath a sky ticking like the clockwork of a bomb; the buildings, the sea—something is cracking, straining. Seagulls lift off from the cliff, cyclists breeze by, a few waves give way. He opens his mouth: the beautiful people are arriving, the biggest international stars come here to carry on their love affairs. He feels as though he were talking to display mannequins. The guy has taken the little girl's hand. Off they go, the two of them. There was a kiss, a handshake, the woman is still here; her sorbet drips in pink plops to the ground, and occasionally on the full, dark skirt the wind, with an effort, is lifting up just a little. The ceremony is over, the cliff did not collapse. He wonders if he should call the police. She comes to life now, says goodbye to him, and walks off, throwing her cone into a trash basket fastened to a tamarisk tree.

The city seems like a tracery of landing strips, hundreds of straight, twinkling, crisscrossing strips, a luminous game of jackstraws. The flight attendant has announced their descent; baggage checked through to its final destination goes directly to the next airport on all night flights. She has a two-hour layover, she'll ask the taxi to take the beltway. She now speaks simple and adequate English; she reserved her seat in English at the travel agency and spoke English to the flight attendant. She's in training. When she doesn't have to show her passport, people take her for a foreigner; neither English—because of the accent—nor from here, obviously. In Sydney, she'll find a small job, then she'll travel: the desert, the pillars of red rock, the virgin forest, the blue lagoons, ranches so vast you need several weeks to tour them on horseback, where riders use mirages (adjusting for the heat and time of day) to judge the distance to the next water hole. The rate of skin cancer among the white population is the highest in the world; gaps are opening in the ozone layer. Sinks drain backward because of the Coriolis force. The bush is infested with dingoes, the sea with man-eating sharks, a big canyon crosses Tasmania, land of waterfalls. There are daily flights to Hobart. A tunnel dug through the center of the Earth would come out there, at the antipodes. The plane is landing, she has to put away her guidebook. In the taxi she affects an English accent to give the name of the other airport, for long-distance flights. Her former address is ten minutes away, she's almost surprised to find it intact in her memory. The child must be asleep at this hour. The apartment is dark, illuminated by the gleam of the streetlights; the child breathes softly and evenly, there, at the end of the hall; on the left, there's the other bedroom; opposite, the living room. She would walk silently around, idly stroking the mantelpiece, rumpling a ficus leaf between two fingers, and could pretend, in front of the furniture with its plump shadows, that dust sheets had been thrown over everything. She buys magazines to stock up for the twenty-hour flight, and a jogging outfit in the duty-free shop. Everything is closing. The airport is emptying out, there are only two more departures tonight, hers and one for Buenos Aires. She could have tackled Spanish: the pampa, gauchos. Travelers in saris have stretched out between the baggage carts, kohl smeared beneath their closed eyes. A man smokes, his head nodding over a newspaper displaying on its front page some Asian personage she doesn't recognize. Maintenance workers sweep around the sleepers; paper wrappers flutter. The silence expands, thickened by breathing, sometimes fissured and set jingling by electronic chimes: you expect an announcement, a name launched by a voice saturated with air, a destination, a lost traveler, but you hear only a hissing, an error, a clumsy movement on the part of flight attendants slipping on their coats. The airport fills with rustlings, documents being put away, the clink of glasses being stacked, a step, the slamming of a door, sometimes a laugh, faint chatter among invisible people: the meager atmosphere of a place one is leaving, amplified and made more distant than a world beyond the seas by the indifference of empty loudspeakers.

She gets a coffee from the vending machine, drinks it leaning against a bay window. The runways are deserted and quite brightly lit. A plane taxis slowly by. She plays at squeezing the light between her eye-lashes into more or less blurry stars. A group of retirees walks past, chatting in English; she finishes her coffee, straightens up to follow them. Boarding has begun.

*This book is dedicated
to the memory of Melsene Timsit.*

DATE DUE

JAN 02 2013